JOURNEY TO FO

Power Surge: The Billionaire Club 4

Dixie Lynn Dwyer

MENAGE EVERLASTING

Siren Publishing, Inc.
www.SirenPublishing.com

A SIREN PUBLISHING BOOK
IMPRINT: Ménage Everlasting

JOURNEY TO FORTUNE
Copyright © 2014 by Dixie Lynn Dwyer

ISBN: 978-1-62741-119-6

First Printing: April 2014

Cover design by Les Byerley
All art and logo copyright © 2014 by Siren Publishing, Inc.

Printed in the U.S.A.

PUBLISHER
Siren Publishing, Inc.
www.SirenPublishing.com

DEDICATION

Dear readers,

Thank you for your continued support, and for making my newest miniseries such a success.

Each story in this series has a similar underlying conundrum. Even with all the money in the world, with the capabilities of buying and getting just about anything one desires, money still cannot buy you love.

This newest story in the series tells a tale about three people who yearn to feel whole, to feel connected, and ultimately to be loved. Their journeys to get there are unique and challenging. Hudson and Jagger must learn to look beyond the monetary, and materialistic things in life to open their hearts to their destinies, while Tia Rose must gain enough self-confidence and determination to put her past behind her, achieve what she wants and craves in life, and just live for today, for the moment, in the power of finding herself so she can ultimately find true love.

Enjoy the story, as Tia Rose, Hudson, and Jagger, embark on their journey to fortune.

JOURNEY TO FORTUNE

Power Surge: The Billionaire Club 4

DIXIE LYNN DWYER
Copyright © 2014

Prologue

"You're lying to me again. I know you are, Salvador. Just spit it out. I want to know why you didn't show up last night. I want to know why you're breaking things off with me. I can handle the truth. Stop patronizing me, Goddamn it!" Tia Rose Richman raised her voice in frustration. She couldn't take it any longer.

Salvador was avoiding her. She was tired of his mistreatment and lack of respect. She felt like she was drowning in this relationship. No matter what she did, he wasn't happy. She never should have stayed with him. Slash that. She never should have gotten involved with him. It was just like her relationship with her parents, except Salvador hadn't hit her. Yet.

She paced her bedroom in her small apartment on the East Side of the Village. New York City wasn't what it was cracked up to be. She was mega pissed off. *The fucker stood me up. Again.*

"I don't think that you can. You're a child. You need to grow up," he snapped at her, in that irritating English accent of his. *The fucking snob. Me, grow up? I've been working my ass off since I was twelve, and had a damn paper route, for crying out loud. Now, after college, I'm still doing odd jobs on the weekends to make money. What the fuck does he mean, grow up?*

"I am far from a child. Just because you have a fucking master's degree in psychology does not make you a damn expert in knowing everyone's personalities. You don't know me at all. I am working my way up at Malone's Designs."

"Working your way up, my ass," he snapped at her. "They're using you. You're their damn puppet. You never stand up for yourself. You never speak your mind. You let people walk all over you and it makes me sick. You're weak, Tia Rose, and your boss knows it. Why do you think you keep getting passed up for promotions and that yearly trip to Paris?"

The bastard knew that statement would hurt me. He knows how hard I've worked.

"You know that my designs were stolen."

"Oh, give me a break. Little Miss Missouri is crying again about how hard it is living in New York City, one of the toughest places around."

She felt the tears sting her eyes. He was such a heartless bastard, and he was too old for her.

"I've had it with you putting me down and saying that I'm not good enough. Not for you or for my profession."

"Well, you're not. I'm done with you. I was with another woman last night."

Her heart ached something terrible. It wasn't that she loved Salvador, but he was so good looking, and so many women craved his attention. When he had found her six months ago, standing in the Marquis hotel, unsure of where the conference room was located, he escorted her and swept her off her feet. She had been naive and stupid. Her parents were right. She was a loser. Their hateful comments and the way they always put Tia Rose down filtered through her mind, making her feel worthless. Salvador's words just added to the facts.

"Did you hear me, Tia? I was with another woman last night."

"With Leza? You slept with Leza?" she asked, knowing that blonde Amazon wanted Salvador so badly. She wanted his money, his reputation, and to be escorted around town as his lover, or mistress. Was she considered a mistress because Salvador was with Tia? She had fallen for his charms, was impressed by his money and maturity, but never connected on that deeper level she yearned for. She shook her head as Salvador released his claws.

"She's a real woman. She's strong, sensual, and open to exploration. I know that you have fears, but you're the coldest bitch I ever fucked."

She gasped and felt her blood pressure boiling.

"Are we back to this again, Salvador? Back to your sick fetishes? I don't need a master's degree to see that you're sick in the head. I won't allow you to tie me up and cut me, so that you can get off on your power trip."

"Tia Rose. Don't push me. It was one time. One time I shared a secret with you and how it made me feel empowered. I was thinking that allowing me that control of you would make you feel empowered, too."

"Ha! As if. You want power and control? You have that in your freaking businesses that you own. You always get what you want when you want it. Not everyone is so spoiled. Leza is so great and so sensual? Then keep her. I'll have you know that I'm a very sensual woman. In fact, I wasn't the problem. You and your small penis were. Good-bye, Salvador, and go to hell!"

Tia Rose disconnected the call.

She stared around at her small, elegantly decorated apartment and absorbed the silence. She glanced at the coffee table, and a small box of ripped movie and Broadway show tickets from when she and Salvador went on numerous dates. She was shaking with fury and some fear. Salvador expected respect, and when he was questioned, she experienced his wrath. It wasn't pretty. She had enough verbal abuse at home. It was another reason why she left. She thought about her parents. The fact that her mother allowed her husband to hit her still to this day frightened Tia Rose. Was Salvador capable of hurting her like that?

I know the answer. I've been denying it for months. Of course he is. Look how quickly he dumped me. Now I have no one again. Is being completely alone, cut off from the world, better than withstanding the pain of insults and abuse?

Suddenly the anger and the hatred for his words, his description of her being a coldhearted bitch slowly began to disintegrate. She was single again. Her very first real relationship went down the tubes because of her feelings of inadequacies, her lack of sexual experience, and her body.

She hated her body.

She hated the large breasts, her large ass, and that damn bit of belly that would never flatten. She did crunches and abdominal workouts until she pulled her back out. She wasn't overly fat, just husky, well-built if she lived in the Renaissance Era. Back then, a woman with her voluptuous, well-curved figure would be considered most beautiful, and the kind of woman every man dreamed of. Women with large breasts and large hips were considered goddesses. *Why hadn't Salvador seen me as a goddess?*

The tears rolled down her cheeks as she grabbed the box, the reminder of a man who hardly knew her at all, and who most definitely didn't love her. She walked to the garbage and threw out the box. She needed to get ready for work.

It was over. Salvador made his choice. If Leza was what he found to be sexually stimulating, then so be it. Today, life changed for Tia Rose. Today, she was once again alone in a world obsessed with emaciated women, dominated by the big mouths with the deep pockets, and she was on the bottom. Her mother was right. A rich handsome man wanted one thing and one thing only. She remembered her mother's hateful words when she called to tell her that she had found someone.

He won't stick around, Tia. He wants one thing from you, and I'm sure you gave it up. Why buy the cow when the milk's for free?

Tia Rose thought about that. The words sunk in immediately. Her mother's intentions in insulting her weight and her lack of self-control were enunciated with the words, "Why buy the cow"—*me*—"when you can get the milk for free?" My virginity. My pussy. Well, that asshole never even gave me an orgasm.

She would get through this. Just like she got through leaving Missouri, her broken heart, and her abusive parents. She had to stop with the self-destruction. She was alone in this world. That was the bottom line. There was no sugar-coating it anymore. Alone, miserable, and unloved. Something had to change. What worse could happen to her now?

Chapter 1

Tia Rose was in a hell of a mood. It seemed like her day could get a bit worse after all. As she took the cab, she sat on melted chocolate. At least she hoped that it was chocolate. Disgusted, she tossed the cab driver his fare, told him about the dirty seat, and then proceeded to the front of the office building. She wished she had worn her light sweater. It was a bit chilly. Scratch that, she wished she had worn a black skirt. That would have at least hid the chocolate. She always kept a change of clothes in her office at work. Just in case. So all she needed to do was get past the front desk and hopefully her bosses, Bernadette and Cade Sinclair.

"Good morning, Tia Rose. You are punctual as usual. I hope you don't mind that I arrived for our meeting thirty minutes early. I have a plane to catch, and I want to stop by the store before I head out."

Tia Rose cringed with her head lowered, staring at the floor, and pausing in her tracks. *Shit, fuck, shit.*

Slowly she looked up. Not that she had to. She knew the sound of the very wealthy, charismatic playboy. God, Dante Parrone was gorgeous. He also hung out with only the hottest females around. He complimented her about her green eyes on more than one occasion. But he was only being a flirt, as most millionaires were.

"Oh, Good morning, Mr. Perrone. Um, could you just give me a few moments to settle in?"

"Dante, darling. How are you this morning? Did Tia offer you an espresso or anything?" Bethany Tyler asked. She appeared out of nowhere. *I swear that woman can smell money from a mile away.*

"Ah, Bethany. You look wonderful as always. No, she didn't have a chance to. Tia just arrived," he said.

Tia Rose turned around to head to her office. She bent over to grab the bag she dropped, as she was carrying too much into work as usual.

Is it really bad that my lack of self-confidence has me thinking about the little homemade chocolate biscotti I made yesterday that are sitting in my lunch bag? Oh, dipping it into some fancy coffee from the office coffee bar would be so relaxing right now.

"Tia, I was hoping to meet with you about those designs. Didn't you mention a whole catalog of new furniture concepts you had?" Her boss, Bernadette Sinclair, appeared from the hallway.

"Oh, hello, Dante. How are you, darling?" she asked then kissed the gorgeous specimen of male on each cheek. It was so French and obviously above Tia Rose's low standards. All three of these people completely forgot that she was in the room. She decided to leave them to their fancy-smancy, rich people talk. Well, in Bethany's case, wannabe rich person. Bethany saw dollar signs and had no morals or values whatsoever. She'd spread her legs for any man with money, and she'd stab her own mother in the back if it meant Bethany would be in the spotlight and filled with fortune. She was that bad.

Tia didn't trust her, but unfortunately, Bethany held the position right above her. She was her boss, so Tia had to keep her mouth shut. That was becoming more and more difficult to do lately. That woman really aggravated Tia Rose. She was so pompous, and she had the nerve to continue to steal Tia Rose's ideas.

Well, I'm too much of a wuss to stand up for myself. Just like what Salvador told me on the phone. I will never stand up for myself. I'm weak and I'm a loser.

She heard a gasp and quickly turned around. Now a few other office workers were standing there. Bethany looked downright excited. Her shit-eating grin was so obvious and huge that Tia wondered what could have possibly made the woman smile that way.

One glance at Dante Perrone and his very uncertain expression, and she felt guilty of something. Her boss had her eyebrows scrunched up, and why was she sniffing the air like that?

"Oh, Mrs. Sinclair, don't worry about the catalogue items Tia was speaking of. I have them all organized and ready to present to you, Mr. Sinclair, and the board. We're meeting in thirty minutes, correct?" Bethany asked.

"What? How could you have the catalogue when I created—"

"I think you need to go use the ladies' room, Tia. Perhaps you should have taken a sick day," she said then chuckled as she looped her arm through Dante's. Dante immediately pulled from Bethany and gave Tia a very apologetic look. Tia had no idea what was going on, and then it hit her.

"Oh. Oh my God, you're all talking about my skirt. Oh, there was this cab," she began to say, but then her boss walked away. The others parted, giggling, and Bethany pulled Dante along with him. Tia could hear what she was saying.

"I'll take care of you, Dante. You know that Tia is more like my assistant, and that her ideas come from me, right?"

Shoulders slumped, anger and disgust heavy on her heart, Tia turned around and walked into her small office. She closed the door and dropped her items to the rug.

"I get absolutely no respect whatsoever around here. None. Zilch. Why am I staying?"

Because you need this job to pay the bills. You need to send money to Missouri. You need to stop being such a scaredy-cat and start showing these people who you are and what you're made of. Enough is enough. Those are my designs. My hard work and months of creativity. How can I let that bitch do this to me?

Tia was suddenly filled with so much anger, rage, and disgust at her life and the person she had become that she felt on the edge of an anxiety attack. She was going to lose it.

That's exactly what Bethany wants me to do. She wants me to crawl under a rock and cry, but do nothing. She wants to take credit for my ideas and reap the benefits. That should be Dante on my arm and in my office and me flirting my ass off with him.

Her belly was filled with butterflies. She wasn't a flirt. She had little self-confidence, and her self-esteem was just as minuscule.

Tia Rose walked around her desk, opened the small cabinet, and pulled out another skirt. It was black. Black hid everything. She had twenty minutes before the meeting.

How embarrassed was she going to be when she walked into that board meeting? Everyone would know about the brown stuff on her skirt. Bethany would surely spread the rumor that it wasn't chocolate. She would be the laughing stock of the office.

She quickly pulled off the one skirt and then stepped into the black one. It was slim fitting, and despite what she felt was an unflattering figure, she felt something begin to filter through her. It almost seemed like tiny little vibrations running through her body. Like a tingling sensation, and then the words popped into her head. Salvador's words. His treatment of her the past few months was questionable to say the least. He had used her for sex, plain and simple.

Salvador was a chubby chaser, and she was chubby.

The tears filled her eyes as she shook her head in a lame attempt to block the words running in her mind.

She saw the little yellow sticky notes tagged to her computer. *Send money to Missouri.*

She hit the keys on the keyboard rather hard. She was always sending money to her parents. Parents that didn't love her and that didn't love one another. It was her guilt for leaving. They blamed her brother, William's addiction to alcohol on her. It had been five years since she left. Five fucking years and they blamed her even though she was so many miles away. Her brother was a loser. He still lived with them, and thank God she left. They would have eventually killed her, or perhaps she would have beaten them to the punch.

She felt the anxiety, the fear of her father's strikes against her skin, from afar. She closed her eyes, willed away the tears, the pain, and fear she had. Missouri was behind her, so why was she not cutting ties with them?

Because you have no one. No one loves you here. They don't love you there either, but any attention, negative as it may be, was better than no attention at all.

She swallowed hard then opened up her bank account information, withdrew the thousand dollars, and sent it off to her mother's account. As she hit send, she felt bile rise in her throat. It was making her sick to send them money, but she couldn't stop herself. If she were a day late, he'd call her. He'd hound her until she answered or sent the money. Her father hated her. But he should hate her. She wasn't anything like her mother. She wouldn't stand there and take his abuse anymore. Instead she ran. She got the hell out of town, out of the state, and started her new life. That move had brought on five years of panic attacks. Especially when her father called and demanded the money.

He called it "restitution for having a worthless child like Tia Rose."

The tears burned behind her eyes as she clenched her teeth and forced the feelings away. She was at work. This would be her sole focus now. Work, work, and more work. She exited out of one screen and tried to log onto the main computer.

Her password wasn't working. She tried again, it went through, and she sighed in relief. But when she looked for the files, the ones she created for the new catalogue, they were nowhere to be found. She explored her options. Now either she fucked up big-time and deleted them, or stored them elsewhere by accident, or someone was snooping around her files.

She felt her chest tighten. All the hard work, all the time spent on creating the custom designs.

Bethany, you bitch.

Tia Rose slammed her hands down on the desk. She felt herself begin to choke up. Those insecure feelings of not being good enough, pretty enough, or skinny enough to compete with the likes of women like Bethany hammered through her mind. She felt sick to her stomach, angry and at her wits' end. If she showed up to that board meeting in—

She glanced at the clock, and then checked her watch.

Five fucking minutes! Five minutes?

She was shaking she was so angry.

The phone on her desk rang. She quickly picked it up and cleared her throat as it cracked with emotion.

"Hello?"

"Yes, there's an order of diapers waiting for you in the hallway, Miss Richman. We heard you needed them pronto, so someone is bringing them up right now."

She heard the roar of laughter in the background.

"Who is this?" She shook harder, her temper flaring.

"The entire staff at Malone's," the voice said, and she knew who it was. That twit, Mark.

"Go to hell." She slammed the phone down and laughter filtered through as she hung up.

She ran her hands through her hair. She turned and looked into the mirror by her desk. She paused, shocked at what she saw. It was as if she were seeing the real her, what she had become, for the first time.

Her big green eyes stood out. Not just because of the thick, black eyelashes, but also because of the fire she currently had within them. Her lips were full, and she needed lipstick. She hadn't even had a chance to apply any makeup. The blouse she wore was conservative, plain, but she reached up and undid two buttons. The move instantly made her look sexier.

She smoothed her hands down her hips, pressing the material of the slim-fitting skirt against her hips. She wasn't flabby, per se. She was solid. A size twelve in most clothing, but strong. She worked out a bit. She loved it, but her size and her weight were set. There wasn't anything she could do about it. This was her physique. Her extra large breasts were real. They were full, and finding comfortable bras were a bitch, but her breasts were hers.

She licked her lips.

"You're not ugly. You're not that fat. You just need to believe in yourself and to stand up for what is right. Stop being a loser. Stop being so shy and reserved that life passes you by. Start opening up your mouth and stop being a doormat."

The phone on her desk rang again.

She rolled her eyes.

"Now what?"

What mean joke would they create now? Were the diapers really waiting for her outside her door?

She reached for her purse, pulled out her little compact of makeup, and added a bit of color to her cheeks. *Chubby cheeks.*

She ignored her sour thoughts as best she could.

She added the lip gloss, then some color to her eyelids.

There. That's better.

Straighten out your shoulders. Stand up and be confident. You've worked too hard. You'll get through this meeting, this day, and then be home safe and in your boring little world.

There was a knock at the door.

"Yes."

The door opened. Alexa was standing there.

"Um, Tia, the meeting is getting started."

"Oh. Okay. I'm on my way."

She grabbed her bag and her leather binder with her notepad inside. It had her initials on it. No one bought it for her. No one accepted her accomplishments in the workforce. She bought it herself.

She acknowledged her hard work, while others took credit. She was losing herself and all the control she had gained by leaving her abusive parents. She was going backward.

She paused in the doorway. Alexa looked at her oddly, and Tia Rose shook her thoughts from her mind. No more negativity. Not today. She needed to plant her heels in the floor and halt any further negativity. How was she supposed to be productive if she felt like this?

As she began to exit the room, she turned to look back at it, the smallest office, and the one without a window. What would be sitting on her desk when she returned? Diapers, food, or maybe dog shit?

She shook her head and when she felt the hand on her shoulder, she nearly jumped.

"They're assholes. You're better than they are, and better than Bethany. Remember that," Alexa said then walked back to her reception desk.

Tia took a deep breath, relieved that she seemed to have at least one ally, even if short-lived.

She headed to the meeting room, and for the first time, she entered with her palms itchy and her attitude adjusted.

* * * *

Cade Sinclair looked at his watch and then looked around the boardroom. Everyone was there except for Tia Rose. He felt bad for her. She was such a sweet, shy woman. She had gorgeous green eyes, a great perception of design, and a hard work ethic. But she didn't have a backbone. She never spoke up. She just went along with things. Year after year he passed her up to attend the events in Paris. It was an opportunity to see what new ideas and designs were out there. For the right individual, it would mean stimulating their creativity.

He turned to look at Bethany as Tia Rose entered the room.

Bethany leaned toward Mark, one of the main board members, and whispered then chuckled.

"Sorry, Mr. and Mrs. Sinclair. I had to take care of some files immediately." She shyly swallowed hard then took the last remaining seat, all the way at the end of the table, and far from the front. That was Tia Rose. Shy, unassertive, and like a doormat. But he had a soft spot for her. He felt badly for her somehow, and he gave her a small smile.

"Not a problem, Tia Rose. Shall we begin?" he asked.

The staff began to speak about the new catalogue launching this September. There were some fresh ideas, and despite the fact that Cade and his wife Bernadette thought Tia Rose was creating the photos and designs, Bethany spoke up.

"I have the designs right here. I went as far as creating a mock catalogue, which of course can be tweaked and changed, but I think you'll find my design ideas inspirational and fresh. That's exactly what you and Mrs. Sinclair had asked for." Bethany directed everyone to look at the folders in front of them.

Cade recognized these designs. He knew Tia Rose had created them. He'd gone to see her a few weeks back and entered her office. She was so caught up in her designs that she hadn't heard him enter. He asked for a peek at the pictures and she shyly stood up from her desk and moved out of the way. He recognized most of these. He had been impressed and looked forward to her final presentation.

He looked at Bethany. She was smug and seemed to be celebrating a victory of sorts, but then he looked at Tia Rose. Her eyes were glued to the pages as she flipped through the catalogue. Her face was becoming brighter red.

"These are amazing, Bethany. How did you come up with such fantastic ideas?" Bernadette asked, as she held up one picture of what appeared to be a breakfast nook with three chairs, and a high round wooden table. It appeared Italian in design, and the accents around the small nook were individually inspiring. It was gorgeous.

Bethany smiled, and then lowered her eyes. "You know me. I'm so busy in the office, and then I take my work home. I love working here, and I would be honored to go to Paris so I could enhance some other ideas I have."

Tia Rose looked up, and when she did, Cade immediately braced himself. Was she going to cry? Was she going to leave the room? Was she going to sit there and let her so-called boss take all the credit for her hard work?

He waited.

* * * *

Tia Rose felt her blood pressure rise, her voice get caught up with emotion as she filtered through her own catalogue. That bitch stole everything, including the layout for the catalogue. That was months of her own hard work, not Bethany's. But now, as she debated about speaking up, accusing her boss of stealing her ideas, she heard Bethany mention Paris. This was what all the hard work was about. Tia Rose dreamed of taking a trip to Paris and seeing the new designs emerging. She wanted to add a fresh new look to the business and show the Sinclairs what she was made of. But she was such a pushover. She allowed Bethany and others to shove her down, make light of her, and dismiss her every minute of hard work.

The others were complimenting her and Bethany was thanking them. She hadn't done shit. She hadn't come up with squat.

Tia Rose looked up from the magazine and locked gazes with Bethany. That smug, nasty model was so damn sure she got away with this, and it irked Tia Rose inside. She saw Mark chuckle as if he knew what the real deal was. Everyone probably knew that Bethany stole Tia's ideas. She hated that fact, and mostly, she hated being made a fool of.

As Bethany was asked about a particular design created on an outdoor scene, near the water, and a boating marina. She began to make up a story about a trip to Hawaii, and the color of the ocean in the background.

"Don't you mean Lake George?" Tia Rose asked as she lifted the magazine and showed everyone the picture.

"What?" Bethany asked.

"Lake George. That scene isn't in Hawaii."

"How can you tell me where the scene was? I'm the one who created that catalogue and I know where I shot the pictures," Bethany replied.

Tia Rose raised her eyebrows. "You shot the pictures? You don't even know how to use your iPhone. I set up everything on the phone for you when you got it and you still screw things up."

Bethany gasped. "You're lying."

"You want to talk about lying, honey? Let's talk about lying." Tia Rose stood up and walked the catalogue to the front of the room and to where Bethany sat a few seats down from Bernadette.

She slammed the book down in front of Bethany and turned to another page.

"Where did you take this shot?"

No answer.

"What type of wood is used in the kitchen design?"

"I don't remember. It was months ago."

Tia Rose turned to another page and asked again, and then she began to explain on every page, where every scene was shot and from her own camera.

"I have those pictures on my thumb drive and in a file. If you were smart, instead of a conniving bimbo, when you stole all my designs, all my months of hard work, then you should have taken the photos, too, and brushed up on your geography."

"You're claiming my work as your own? How dare you? I don't have to sit here and take this." Bethany began to rise, and then Tia Rose placed her hand on Bethany's shoulder and smiled wickedly at her. It felt so good.

"Please stay. I think everyone will want to hear about this trip to Hawaii for research to do this scene. That was back in February during the blizzard here in New York, right?" Tia Rose asked, and then turned to another page, where there was a gorgeous winter scene that could be seen through the windows of a formal living room. The fireplace mantel was Tia Rose's design.

She slammed her hand down on the magazine.

"These are my ideas, my concept, my creations, and not yours."

"Tia Rose. That is quite the allegation," Mrs. Sinclair stated.

"Bernadette, be quiet. Let Tia Rose state her case," Cade stated. Tia Rose felt her cheeks warm. She looked around the room. She saw the stunned expressions. None of them would believe her. They would believe Bethany.

"Mrs. Sinclair, I mean no disrespect when I say this, but if you think Bethany created these designs and worked for months to come up with a mock catalogue on her own, then you're not as in tune to your loyal employees as I always thought you were."

Bernadette gasped. Cade smiled.

"She's out of her mind. She should be fired," Bethany stated.

Tia Rose took a deep breath and looked around the room. "You all know about the lies, the practical jokes, and mean and hurtful things Bethany has done to me since I started working for Malone's. But you also know Bethany. Who is the one who is always staying late, never taking vacation time, and always there to help each and every one of you when you drop the ball, fall short with your deadlines, or need a bit of creative advice?"

She looked at them then pointed to herself.

"Me."

"She's insane. She shouldn't be here," Bethany stated.

"Maybe we should call security," Mark suggested.

"Don't bother. I quit. But I'm taking my catalogue, my pictures, and my hard work along with me. If you try to steal my ideas, I'll slap a lawsuit on your tiny stuck-up ass so fast you won't know what hit you. And I can do that. Because I edited every picture, design, and concept in this magazine. You should learn how to do the job you've been getting paid nearly two Gs to do, Bethany. Kiss my ass."

Tia Rose felt so triumphant that she wanted to fist pump and scream "hell yeah." But as she grabbed her bag and scooped up the catalogue, not bothering to look around, she heard the others begin to speak as Bernadette demanded that she stay. She turned to listen. Everyone was making comments, admitting that Tia Rose helped them all along and they knew Bethany was using her. Everyone knew that Bethany continued to steal Tia's ideas.

Then Mr. Sinclair spoke up.

"Everyone quiet down, and, Tia Rose, please sit back down."

Everyone did as he said but Tia remained standing.

"I won't stay, sir. I won't stand here and continue to be used. I can't stand the jokes, the nastiness, and backstabbing. I'm not that kind of person. If that's the type of employees you want here at Malone's, then I think I should hand in my resignation and look for a job elsewhere." As she said the words, her belly did a series of deep twists and turns. She felt like vomiting, which would totally kill her triumphant moment of standing up to Bethany and telling her off.

Bernadette leaned over to her husband and whispered into his ear. Just then security entered the room. Someone had called them.

Oh my God, I'm going to be escorted out of the meeting and probably out of the building. I'll be fired, I'll have no job, and I won't be able to pay that stupid rent. I won't be able to send the money to my parents. He'll kill me. He'll haunt me every hour of every day until I send that money. Oh my God, why did I do this?

"Thank you for coming so quickly. Please remove Miss Tyler from the room. Escort her to her office, have her clean out her desk, and then accompany her outside of the building. She is no longer an employee here."

Bethany gasped as the two security men approached.

"I don't believe this. I can't believe that you would take that fat bitch's side over mine. I fit here. I have style, class, and a great body. She's fat, has no spine, and wouldn't know what to do in the presence of designers," Bethany stated.

"Remove her," Mr. Sinclair repeated.

Bethany shoved the catalogues that were in front of her across the table and she began to have a tantrum.

Tia Rose wasn't too shocked. Once the room was cleared, Bernadette and Cade smiled at her.

"Please have a seat, Tia Rose. It's so nice of you to have finally joined us. We have a lot to discuss, including your upcoming trip to Paris."

Tia Rose was shocked speechless. *Nice of me to show up? He knew all along. He was waiting for me to grow a spine and stand up for myself.*

"Thank you, sir. It's nice to finally show up and let you all know what I'm made of."

"This is going to be great," one of the other staff stated. Then they all congratulated her and told her how proud they were of her. It was an utter and complete turnaround. They began to ask questions about the designs and her ideas, and the Sinclairs had questions of their own. Tia Rose answered them with confidence and obvious knowledge, proving further what she was capable of, despite not being a super thin model like Bethany.

This was a new beginning. The new Tia Rose. There were more changes to come. She just knew it as she pointed to the scenes, described the materials used, and expanded on her ideas. They all listened to her intently.

Watch out, world, here I come.

Chapter 2

Hudson Ross sat in the recliner on his private jet and sipped his dirty martini. He was on the satellite phone with his twin brother, Jagger, wondering when he would arrive in Paris. Hudson had been to Milan first, and now was headed to France. It had been a crazy few weeks, and he looked forward to getting back to the States and working on their new renovations to one of their vacation homes.

Their friends, Flynn and Jett, had called him numerous times wondering when he would be joining them for poker night again. He had to laugh. That weekly get-together had been great. He thought that maybe since Nash and Riker, Cash and Zane, and Emerson and Stone were in serious relationships, that things would change. But they hadn't. The only thing that changed was Jagger and Hudson's new increased desire to find their perfect woman. She was out there somewhere. It seemed that his brother Jagger was working on finding her fast instead of letting fate step in. He chuckled to himself.

"Sorry, I can't hear you. What did you say?" Hudson asked.

"I said, I'm in the middle of something. I got a good shot at this woman. I may be later on Sunday than I first thought," Jagger said then chuckled.

"Quit it, man. Get out here by Sunday."

"Why? I've been to plenty of these fashion events. They're all the same. Tiny food made for the birds, assholes throwing around their money, and skinny, near anorexic chicks trying to look sexy."

"We're not doing this for the models. We're doing this for the furniture, and to get ideas. I haven't liked one thing I saw from all the known designers. It's both of our decision, bro. We're in this together, just like everything else," Hudson said.

"Well, will you at least try to make it worth my while? It's a long flight and I have to leave late Saturday."

"I promise a special little something will be here waiting for you when you arrive."

"Voluptuous, hips and ass, and no skin and bones?"

"Voluptuous, just the way we both like them."

"I'll see what I can do. But tonight's a different story. Later, bro."

Jagger hung up and Hudson laughed.

It would be great if one day they found that perfect, sexy woman they yearned to share. She just didn't seem to exist, and instead, they settled. It was getting boring. Hudson wanted something different. He wanted companionship and he wanted it sooner rather than later.

He was sick of the nightclubs, except for The Phantom. That was different. That was their best friends' place. It was where they could chill out, not have to stand in the spotlight, walk the damn red carpet, or supply the dough to run the parties.

He enjoyed the nightlife to an extent. But he preferred running the businesses, even though he had people to do it for him and Jagger. He shook his head and smiled as he thought about Jagger. His twin was nearly a complete opposite of him. Jagger liked speed and adrenaline rush. If there was a dare or challenge to meet, Jagger was on it like white on rice. The man got himself into more complicated situations than Hudson could keep up with. He never led with his heart. He kept it locked up, and that was something they both shared.

He sighed as he felt almost sad inside at the admission, even if it were in thought. Had money truly kept them from being more caring, and perhaps trusting?

Hell, yeah. Everyone wants everything Jagger and I have. As soon as they learn I'm a billionaire, they clasp on and I need the Jaws of Life to get them off. Nope, I don't need the hassle of opening up my heart. Not unless that special someone suddenly arrives. Yeah, not happening to me.

Hudson glanced at his Rolex and saw he had at least two more hours before he landed. He was excited about seeing some new designs and attending the gala. He was hoping to meet some of the designers whose work he admired in the magazines he saw. Yet, he worried about their personalities. A lot of the designers were snobs or the people who represented them were. If they heard he had money, they would up the price. He needed to be suave. Maybe pretend he wasn't in the market to buy, but browse instead? Whatever. He would make the decision as soon as he saw the prospects.

Closing his eyes, he leaned back in the recliner, and hoped that this trip wasn't a waste of time. Money, he had an abundance of. That was his least worry. But lately he was feeling as if money wasn't the most important thing anymore. Sure he had all the fancy cars, the multiple houses, and could buy anything or anyone he wanted. Not that he ever did that, but knowing he had the power to do so boosted his male ego. He smirked to himself. Nah, something was bothering him. He just hadn't been feeling right lately. He felt a bit hollow inside, and he wondered why.

Maybe he just needed to loosen up. Perhaps find a beautiful, sexy woman to get lost in for an evening, or even the weekend?

With thoughts of hooking up and easing that hollow feeling, Hudson fell asleep.

Chapter 3

Tia Rose stood on the balcony of her room at one of the most luxurious hotels in France. She sipped her wine, enjoying the amenities of her room at the Trianon Palace Versailles. The room's décor was gorgeous. Rich purples accented the sheer white curtains and king-sized bedding. Even the rug throughout the suite had a purple, cream, and black unique pattern going through it. Some of the accent pieces, like the bench, the headboard, and upholstered chairs were done in rich, dark plum velvet, which made them stand out among the whites. She felt the warm, gentle breeze, as she leaned against the open glass patio doorway. The sheer white curtains danced slightly in the breeze and she could smell the abundant aroma of flowers from the garden below.

"I'm in Paris, France. I'm in an executive suite fit for a princess," she said aloud, then giggled before taking another sip of the French wine.

She could see the fields of green grass in the distance, the air crisp and clean and almost magical. Something stirred inside of her. Life was just beginning for her now, at age twenty-four.

She glanced toward the bedside table, noting the time, and the need to get ready for tonight's event. Instead of roaming through the displays today, as the vendors and craftsman set up, she'd decided to venture off into the city, and find the local artists and what they had to offer. It had been a complete inspiration, as she stopped along the way and drew her own designs, with ideas stemming from what she saw.

Of course people's tastes were always so different in America, but in New York, the influences of various countries and cultures were accepted and received well.

The Sinclairs were already impressed with the e-mails and pictures she had sent in the last few days. Tonight and the rest of the weekend were hers to enjoy.

She closed the doors to the balcony, locked them, and then stepped down into what was the master bedroom. She grabbed her dress, the one she'd purchased at a lovely boutique about twenty kilometers from Versailles, in Paris. It was a bit expensive, but as she splurged on getting her hair done here, along with a waxing, which led to a manicure and pedicure, she was ready for tonight.

It was crazy, but as she exited the salon, even dressed casually in another outfit she'd purchased in Versailles, she felt sexy, beautiful, and alive. People seemed to notice her immediately. She was so glad she'd splurged, but as she stared at the dress, she began to second-guess the woman at the boutique.

The dress was slim fitting, and totally accentuated her large breasts. Amazingly, she had been so nervous before leaving for Paris, she actually slimmed down a little. Not that she was skinny or even remotely close. She never would be. That was a fact about her body type, but she looked good. She was firm in all the right places and soft where she should be. It made her feel beautiful.

Then, of course, the dressmaker at the boutique talked her into buying some sexy French lingerie. Even after explaining that she was single, and absolutely not in the mood to get involved with another man, the woman spouted words about destiny and the magic of Versailles.

Tia Rose stared at the dress. *Perhaps it is a bit too much.*

She downed the rest of the glass of wine. She felt her body relax a little.

"Oh, well, I'm in Paris. I don't know a soul, and I'm leaving in four days."

She took a step forward and felt her body move seductively across the carpet.

Her confidence was rising despite the years of doubt and lack of self-confidence. She kept repeating the words, "This is the new you."

"Tonight I live for the moment, for the pleasure of happiness, with no worries, no denials and fears. I will embrace whatever comes my way."

* * * *

Hudson Ross was walking through the gala. He had to admit that he wasn't too impressed with what he saw on display. He also didn't care for some of the people making their way through the event and appearing stuck-up. He was looking at a set of furniture, way overpriced and sort of ugly, if he was being honest. But as he eyed a single standing cabinet, he caught sight of something much more appealing.

It was odd, but her hair, and then the sound of her sweet laughter as she spoke with one of the vendors were what initially drew his eyes toward her. Her back was turned toward him, and Hudson wondered if the front of her was as appealing as the back. Her hips were curved. The dress she wore was snug against them then flared toward the bottom to her calves. She wore black high heels that had a thin stripe of purple on the heel of each shoe. Her legs were gorgeous.

The back of the purple dress was lined on the edges of her skin with a matching purple line of fabric. It appeared to be made of silk, and he assumed she must have purchased it at a local shop in Paris. There was a unique French flair to it. Her skin was creamy and her shoulders bare as well. He couldn't take his eyes off of her, as one of the waiters smiled, winked, and then handed her a glass of wine. She tried to decline, the waiter made a comment Hudson couldn't hear, but she laughed and then took the fancy glass.

She turned to look around, and like a punch to his gut, he felt himself flinch inside.

Oh, my God. She's perfect.

Her gaze filtered through the room, as if trying to determine which way she should go next. He absorbed the way the designer dress fit her like a glove, yet revealed enough cleavage to make a man like him fall to his knees and beg for her attention. She was a goddess. A Renaissance woman, and he knew he needed to find out more about her. He had to, before some other man or men claimed what belonged to him.

He was shocked at the immediate possessive thoughts. He was acting like an ass. Just because he felt confident that he could get any woman he wanted, didn't mean that this one would automatically accept him. Or perhaps she would. He wasn't sure and he didn't want to waste time overthinking this. He was a natural. He was thirty years old, experienced, and a billionaire who fought with the toughest of CEOs in business board meetings. Surely he could seduce a beautiful woman with a body his cock seemed enticed by.

He followed her, and when she stopped by a set of porcelain dishes sitting on some designer tables, he spoke to her.

"That is quite a stunning piece. Do you collect?" he asked her. She abruptly turned toward him, and he felt his eyes zero in on her gorgeous green eyes. The woman was a knockout. She looked sweet as she stumbled to reply to him. He looked her face over as he gave a small smile.

She had the face of a porcelain doll. She smelled as edible as she looked.

"I don't. I was just browsing." Her American, maybe Northeast accent mixed with a bit of Southern twang, alerted him immediately to the fact that she was not French. Did she live here? Was she visiting? Was she here with someone?

"Oh, I was going to tell you that the prices here are high. There are better places in town and beyond, near the villages."

"Oh, I know. I went through some of them the last few days. You're not French, are you?" she asked. He gave a small smile as a group of browsers cleared their throats as if he and this lovely woman were in their way. They held one another's gazes for a moment and then she smiled. He felt it straight to his gut. This was different. He needed to know her. He would totally get to know her.

He reached for her elbow and stepped with her to the side. His heart pounded and his blood heated. She felt amazing. The attraction was mesmerizing.

"I'm not French, no. Are you?" he asked, and she shyly turned away and looked toward the side and another table of merchandise.

"No," she replied as he walked along with her, and toward the large dining area inside.

He wasn't going to leave her, but he didn't want to seem pushy.

"So, is this your first trip to Paris?" he asked.

She looked at him, her eyes wide as saucers as she stared at his face. Was she liking what she saw? He wondered, and then smiled. She was speechless, and he thought she couldn't get any more beautiful.

She took a sip of wine and wet her lips by sticking out her tongue. He was wrong. She kept getting more beautiful.

"It is my first trip here, and you?"

"Oh, no, I've been here before."

"With business?"

He wasn't going to give her much information. He needed to learn more about her. He stepped closer, his need to inhale her scent and let her know his intentions, obvious.

"You are so stunning. What is your name?" he asked.

She nearly gulped.

"Tia Rose," she replied. He had to bite his lip between his teeth to not moan in pleasure. "That's a gorgeous name, Tia Rose. A lovely name for a lovely woman." He let his eyes roam over her cleavage.

"Are you meeting anyone, or would you like to accompany me to the dining area? I'm dining alone," he added suddenly, and it shocked him. This woman was the first woman to make him feel nervous.

She studied him for a moment, and then took another sip of wine. Was it liquid courage?

"Okay. I'm alone, too, so this will be nice. What's your name?"

"Hudson."

"Nice to meet you, Hudson," she whispered, and then stuck out her hand. As he took her hand into his own, he felt a shock of awareness.

He whispered next to her ear, as he inhaled her sensual perfume. "I must tell you, Tia Rose, you are a very stunning woman."

Her cheeks turned a nice shade of pink, and then she lowered her eyes. *A true submissive.*

He felt his cock press against the zipper of his tuxedo pants. This woman was special, and tonight was going to be his best night ever in Paris.

* * * *

Tia Rose prayed to God that she wouldn't make an ass of herself.

The man escorting her along the hallway with his arm looped through hers was serious eye candy. She could feel the bulging muscles beneath his tuxedo jacket, and God, he smelled incredible, too. She swallowed hard and nearly tripped. She shouldn't have had that third glass of wine. Not that she finished it, but she wasn't used to drinking, and she also wasn't used to men like this paying attention to her.

Sure, since she'd arrived in Paris, she'd felt more alive and beautiful than ever before. It was like life didn't exist before now. She knew that sounded silly, but she wanted to hold on to the fantasy for as long as she could.

She looked up at him. The man was at least six feet four inches tall. He had to be. She was wearing high heels, and she still was short. He looked like a disciplinary, with his short, crew-cut hair, deep hazel eyes, and an air about him that signified power, control, and natural sex appeal. Her damn pussy came alive, and she actually felt her panties get wet. She was getting off on this stranger from his looks alone. It was shocking, and she tried to give herself a mental kick in the ass, but it was no use. The man was hot.

As they made their way through the dining area, she could see all the major industry people chatting and trying to sell their products. She was glad she wasn't here to sell products. This was her time now.

"How is this table over here, Tia Rose? It's a little more private, and has a nice view of the city streets below."

"Yes, that one is perfect," she said, and could hear her voice shaking. Her palms were sweaty and she wondered if this man were for real. Had the wine gone to her head? Was she imagining this?

He pulled the chair out for her to sit. She smiled, and when she took the seat he offered and looked up to inhale his cologne one last time before he sat down, he squeezed her shoulder. The chills of awareness and desire shot through her system. Her nipples tightened, as if there were an imaginary string from where his hands squeezed to her nipples. *Holy shit.*

What the hell is happening to me? I want this man. I want to get lost in his eyes, in his huge embrace, and underneath him.

She felt her cheeks flush at her perverted thoughts. God, she needed more experience.

Get it with Hudson. Get it here in Paris.

Immediately a waiter arrived and took their drink orders while passing them menus. Hudson ordered a bottle of some fancy French wine. It must have been costly because the waiter raised his eyebrows at him and suddenly seemed to want to cater to Hudson's every need.

Hudson smiled at her from across the table.

"Do you know a lot about wine?" she asked, trying to steer the conversation away from what was really on her mind.

Are you married? Do you have a girlfriend? Are you a serial killer? Do you want to have sex with me tonight no strings attached?

She gulped hard, and then looked down at the menu again. He began to speak about the wine in Paris and how this particular wine he ordered was from a local winery, which had existed for centuries. She found herself mesmerized by the tone of his voice. It was commanding, yet comforting and firm. When he spoke, she listened to every word. He was that charismatic and powerful. It made her shiver with trepidation, yet aroused her nipples. She hoped the dress covered the not-so-tiny buds. Being well-endowed and then some, her aroused nipples would surely show through the satin. She moved her arms and used the large menu to block his view as she tried to caress away the ache. When she looked up at him, and the fact that he seemed to watch her knowingly, she felt embarrassed.

He reached the short distance across the table and took her hand.

"I feel it, too. Let's enjoy dinner and then see where things lead."

She was stunned to silence. She couldn't speak. The man was a master at seduction and knowing a woman's body. He probably did shit like this all the time. So why wasn't she running for the nearest exit?

Because he is that fine. He has the most amazing, sexy eyes, and his dominance and experience are a total turn-on. Let's see what you have, lover boy. Will he take a chance on me, a plus-size female? Oh, boy, does my pussy sure hope so.

* * * *

"This is delicious," she stated, and Hudson watched her as she enjoyed a second glass of the wine. She was easing up, but she was still so shy and reserved. When she told him they shouldn't share too much information about one another, he was shocked. He was the man here. He thought he was leading the way to getting to know her, and hopefully having her in his bed this evening, but Tia Rose surprised him. It seemed she was just as attracted to him as he was to her.

They ate their meal in little silence. One conversation led to another, and soon they were sharing dessert and staring at one another across the table. It was getting late, but time seemed to not matter at all. He no longer focused on her being in his bed as he did on listening to her voice, her ideas about Paris, and the world. She was associated with some sort of business, but as he asked more questions, she evaded the answers.

He did find out that she worked in design. By her extensive knowledge of furniture, ceramics, and materials, she seemed to be involved with the industry this gala was hosting tonight. He was a good judge of character. Hudson needed to be, for business as well as pleasure. It was especially important to read the signs and the body language of a person he was spending time with. Tia Rose seemed reserved and shy, yet the dress she wore, the style of her hair, and the light amount of makeup on her, all indicated something entirely different than what he was getting from conversing with her.

Perhaps she just dressed up so much for this evening, and for the simple fact that she was in Paris. What was really peculiar about this encounter was the fact that she didn't want to know a thing about him. Not if he were rich or poor, just whether he was married or single or lived here in Paris. She seemed disappointed when he said he didn't live here, yet she stopped him from saying where it was he lived. She intrigued him, and the more they talked, and the more wine they drank, the easier conversation flew, as well as time.

Then he began to wonder what his twin brother, Jagger, would think of her. He almost felt like he didn't want to share her. Or maybe it was that he feared she wouldn't be compatible to both of them. He wasn't sure, so he embraced tonight, and what was surely yet to come.

* * * *

Tia Rose laughed at something Hudson told her. She was having an amazing time. To think that she actually almost walked away from Hudson when they first met was crazy. It also would have been one of the stupidest decisions of her life. Then she reminded herself that this was the new her. She didn't know this man. She didn't even tell him where she was from, or ask where he was from. They settled on the Untied States as their answer.

He was charming and as big as an NFL linebacker, and he carried himself well. In front of him she actually felt feminine and petite. It was crazy. *Me, feminine and petite. No one ever made me feel this beautiful, this attention getting.*

The bread and cheeses were divine, but she couldn't seem to eat too much. She knew she should, especially drinking so much wine, but she felt so comfortable and relaxed. She could get lost in his gorgeous hazel eyes, and manly expressions.

"Shall we walk outside?" he asked her as the evening was drawing later and later. She didn't know what time it was, just that she was getting tired, yet felt energetic at the same time.

"Where are you staying?" he asked.

"Not far from here." It was how she played out most of their conversation. She didn't want him to know too much about her, and he seemed to not want to reveal too much about himself.

When he took her hand to pull her out of the way of some pedestrians walking, he escorted her to a private garden area. There were fountains and greenery, and the light was dim. Right before she bent to take a seat, Hudson pulled her into his arms. Somehow, she fit perfectly. He cupped her cheek with his hand, and stared down into her eyes. His other hand remained against her lower back, and partially over her ass.

I want his hands on my ass. I want to feel his large hands all over me.

"Tia Rose, you are such a beautiful woman. I've enjoyed the evening so much. I don't want it to end. Come back to my hotel with me. Come spend the night in my arms?" he asked.

She wasn't as shocked as she thought she would be. Or maybe as she should be. Instead she smiled, and he leaned down and kissed her lips softly.

His lips were firm and his kiss somewhat gentle. As she kissed him back and he drew her closer, using his hand to cover part of her ass cheek while pressing her against him, a hunger greater than anything she felt before arose within her.

She wanted this man. Hell, if they owned the garden, she'd let him have her right here. The feeling of desperation was remarkable.

He pressed his tongue between her teeth and deepened the kiss. When she felt his hand attempt to cup her breast, she moaned into his mouth. Nothing ever felt like this. Not a touch, not a comment, not even an embrace from someone who cared, felt like this.

She had gotten so used to being alone, and not feeling complete or loved, she could hardly recognize this feeling for what it was. An attraction, lust, or just chemistry? She didn't care. She wanted more. She needed more. This was a new Tia Rose. No running in fear. No second-guessing her abilities. No, tonight she lived for herself, for the need burning inside of her, and for whatever Hudson could bring her in one night of pleasure.

As Hudson slowly released her lips, their foreheads pressed close, and he smiled down at her.

"You are everything I've ever wanted in a woman."

She gulped and wondered if it were just a line. The feelings of reservation emerged, but her newfound confidence and desire to be strong and self-confident reemerged stronger.

"We better head to your hotel, Hudson, before I change my mind."

His eyes seemed to darken with desire as he gripped her hand and began to walk her rather quickly from the gardens. She nearly lost her balance, due to the combination of too much wine, and the hypnotic spell of Hudson she was under.

This was it. She was going to have sex with a man she hardly knew at all, yet who made her feel more alive than any other person she had met in her twenty-four years of life.

Chapter 4

They walked hand in hand, kissing along the way, as if they were already lovers. The warm night air caressed her skin and shoulders as they took the small trip to The Villa Hotel Majestic. It was a five-star hotel with amazing amenities, mostly known for the spa treatments and rich ambiance.

The inside of the main lobby was stunning. Lots of glass, unique bold patterns, and designs she was becoming accustomed to, and of course, a personalized greeting.

She was so caught up in looking around the main lobby as Hudson escorted her to a private elevator. As soon as they were inside, despite being accompanied by a hotel employee who operated the elevator, Hudson cornered her. His hands caressed her hips, and his mouth took possession of her own. She didn't have a care in the world until the elevator doors opened, and the doorman cleared his throat.

He smiled wide at them. Hudson tipped him and then exited the elevator. There was only one room on this wing. She saw the words on the gold plate. *Executive Suite.*

As he used his key card to unlock the door, she felt her belly do a series of twists and turns. Was she going through with this? She didn't know this man at all.

He closed the door, pulled her into his arms, and pressed her hard against the door.

She gasped. He held her gaze, looked over her breasts and back to her face again.

"I feel so damn wild with need. It's incredible. You do this to me, Tia Rose."

His mouth covered hers, and the man took complete control of her body and her soul.

She wondered if he would take her right there against the door. It wouldn't matter to her. She was so aroused and wet. But instead, he eased back slightly to lick across her neck and her cleavage then back up again.

His mouth was against her earlobe. He pulled it into his mouth between his teeth and pulled gently.

"Touch me. Please, touch me," he whispered.

He sounded so desperate. Like he really wanted her and needed her or he would lose it. It was exactly how she felt about him. She pushed thoughts of Salvador, her one and only lover from her mind. He knew nothing about how to treat a woman and make her feel desired. Hudson was a pro, and she would relish in every sensation he gave her. Even if it were only for tonight.

She ran her hands up his tuxedo, and shoved the jacket away from his shoulders.

He only moved his hands from her body for a moment, to shake the jacket off.

It fell to the floor, and he grabbed her again, this time slipping his hand under her dress as he licked across her cleavage.

"Open for me, goddess. Let me feel that wet pussy of yours."

Holy shit.

She moaned from his words alone, felt the cream fill her panties as she spread her feet apart, and welcomed his touch. She needed it. She wanted it so badly her pussy lips ached with need.

"Yes, oh God, Hudson, this is crazy."

His fingers connected with her panties. "It is wild, crazy. I want you. I want you spread out on my bed where I can explore this voluptuous body of yours. You're perfect. You're beautiful. You're all mine." His fingers plunged up into her cunt.

"Oh, Hudson." She gripped his shoulders, nearly ripping his shirt from his body. His mouth covered hers. He pressed his tongue in and out of her mouth, exploring her cavern deeply, while his fingers plunged similarly into her needy pussy.

She felt her body tighten and knew she was going to come. She wanted to holler to the Gods, and thank them for sending her here to Paris to meet Hudson, and to feel his fingers draw out her juices in pleasure.

She was panting and absorbed everything. The way she kicked back her heel against the door for leverage to pump her hips against his thick, hard fingers. She pressed her breasts forward, ran her fingers through his crew-cut hair, and kissed him deeply back.

What a sight she must look like. Hair a mess, dress up to her waist, garters showing and Hudson's fingers disappeared between her slick folds.

She never felt so damn sexy in her entire life.

"Oh, oh, Hudson, I'm coming."

He pulled his fingers from her cunt, and she gasped as she gripped his arms so she wouldn't fall.

He pulled her to him. "Not here. In bed. My bed, where you belong."

When he scooped her up as if she weighed hardly anything at all, the tears hit her eyes, her throat closed up, and she gasped.

Oh, my God, I'm in love.

Holy fucking shit, he's carrying me. He isn't struggling at all. He's strong, he's handsome, he's sexy as anything, and he wants me. He wants me, Tia Rose, size twelve, voluptuous woman.

He placed her feet down on the rug at the end of the king-size bed. She barely had time to look around the room at the décor, but she was so interested in that. There were bold garnet-covered chairs, velvet tapestries in rich black and white designs and there were numerous rooms. A damn large place for one man to be staying alone.

He cupped her face with his thick hands and stared at her lips.

"How lucky I was to find you." He kissed her softly and then turned her around to face the bed.

It was big, and she would be lost within it. The comforter was thick white, with a bedspread folded on the bottom in a strong, luxurious ruby red.

She felt his knuckles caress her shoulders, then down her spine. He began to unzip her dress, and in a flash, it began to fall. On instinct, she grasped the bodice and turned toward him. She was scared out of mind. The fear and the lack of self-confidence were winning the battle within. What if he thought she was bigger than she appeared? What if he didn't like the swell of her belly, the size and shape of her breasts, or her big ass?

She wanted to run.

"Hudson, maybe this isn't—"

He covered her lips with one finger, and stared down into her eyes. "Baby, you are perfect. Your eyes are the greenest I have ever seen. Your lips and your smile are so enticing, and I could just hold you in my arms and kiss you for hours."

She lowered her eyes, wondering if his words were true or if he were trying to make her feel better.

He gripped her around the waist and hoisted her against his large, muscular chest.

His fingers caressed her cheeks. His touch was soft and he had her complete attention.

"Trust me. Trust that I want you. I want to be lost inside of you, and bring you nothing but complete pleasure. Your body is exceptional, and like a woman with strength, conviction, desire, and confidence from an era, that fills my fantasy. You turn me on." He thrust his hips against her mound, and she felt his thick, long cock.

She stared at him, the sincerity in his eyes, and the seriousness in his face.

I could fulfill this God's fantasy?

Then his eyes grew almost darker, as she slowly released her dress. The dress fell to the rug, and Hudson stared at her in awe and admiration.

She thought she would pass out in excitement when he fell to his knees before her.

His hands moved swiftly over her skin, to the waist of her panties. Now she was silently thanking the dressmaker who insisted she get the fancy lingerie. He caressed them down her body, then leaned forward and kissed her belly. Thank God she had gotten the waxing, too.

He kissed her right where that unmanageable swell of her tummy stood out slightly over her groin. Then he looked up at her.

"I have particular tastes, Tia Rose. A man used to being in charge and getting whatever it is I want. I want you. Sit on the bed, spread your thighs, and offer me your pussy."

Oh. My. God!

* * * *

Hudson could tell that Tia Rose was self-conscious, but he didn't know why. She was solid, she was curvy in every place it mattered, and she fit him perfectly. As she stared at him a moment after his statement, he wondered if she would run like hell.

He caressed her inner thighs slowly, and as she licked her lips and released an unsteady breath, she widened her thighs.

He was utterly thrilled at the sight.

"You're beautiful everywhere. Especially here." He caressed a finger against her glistening, wet folds. She shook and reached for his wrist and tried to close her legs.

"No." His word was firm and she immediately halted. He held her gaze. Her face, like that of an angel, stared at him. Her green eyes sparkled, she licked her lips, and he felt the cream drip from her pussy.

She was turned on. He raised his eyebrow at her and she lowered her chin to her chest.

"Show me what is mine tonight. Offer me everything and nothing less, Tia Rose."

Slowly she parted her thighs, placed her hands to the side, and he moved in for a taste of her cream.

Her head fell back, her breasts, still confined by the sexy lace bra, tilted forward. He wanted to see more of her.

He was utterly thrilled to feel her tight little cunt suck his fingers in. He stroked her gently, but all he wanted to do was shove his dick into her and fuck her until she was completely satiated. He shook the possessive, wild thoughts from his mind and focused on Tia Rose's needs.

She was sweet, she was shy, and she was perfect.

"You're so wet, baby. You like the way this feels?" he asked.

"Yes," she replied instantly.

"Take off your bra. I want you naked."

She looked at him and he stroked her cunt a little faster. She opened her mouth to moan and then thrust against his digits. He leaned forward and nipped her pussy.

She arched and thrust forward.

"You are so sexy and you feel so tight, baby. I want to be sure you're slick and wet for me. I'm a big man."

She reached back and began to undo her bra, and a hunger like no other began to emerge.

He curled a finger, finding that special spot, deep within her. She panted, and moaned, as he applied more pressure.

"Oh, Hudson. What is that—"

She shook and exploded against his fingers. The sloshing sound filled the room, and he had waited long enough.

Hudson stood up and began to strip.

* * * *

She couldn't move. Whatever the hell he just did, he caused the dams to open and she wanted more.

As he removed his clothes and all his thick, bulging muscles came into view, she panicked.

He must have realized she was going to evade him because his arm snaked out and caught her.

"I asked you to trust me. I know I'm big, but you can handle me. You're meant to be mine." He cupped her cheeks and kissed her. She instantly lost the tension in her body and eased against him. She ran her hands over the solid, wide muscles and then to his ass.

He chuckled when she gave his cheeks a squeeze. She could get very used to exploring his body, too.

"Are you on the pill?" he asked, and she nodded her head. She wanted to have children. Salvador didn't want any. He made her go to the doctor and get protection. He told her it was her responsibility, not his.

She locked gazes with Hudson, who now held her against him and stared into her eyes.

He was nothing like Salvador.

He brushed a strand hair away from her cheek.

"You are so serious, Tia Rose. I wonder what thoughts are traveling through that brain to make you look so scared."

His bare cock pressed against her belly.

"Forget anything but me." He kissed her again. In a flash he lifted her up and placed her on the bed. His thigh was between her thighs. She reached for the thigh-high stockings and he stopped her.

"They stay on. You look sexy." He pressed his chest lower over hers and kissed her. His mouth felt hot and amazing against her flesh. She felt sexy and alive, and she wanted to give Hudson whatever he wanted. She didn't care. She was living for tonight, for now.

His mouth trailed lower over her neck then to her chest. He cupped her breasts. She looked down and was surprised at how his large hands nearly covered a good portion of them.

He stroked her nipples, rolled them between two fingers, and then pulled.

She reached for his hand as she gasped from the sensations.

"It's too much. I never felt like this before."

"Place your hands above your head. Do not move them, Tia Rose, unless I tell you."

His words were firm. He was ordering her around in bed, and she loved it.

"Remember the rules." He twirled her nipple between his fingers as he lay half over her body.

She raised her arms up. The move caused her breasts to tilt upward, and he used the opportunity to lick the tip, and suck part of her breast into his mouth.

She was never so turned on in her entire life. This man, his words, his commands, and this entire situation were outrageous. But it fed a hunger, a need inside so great, it made her come again.

The man was relentless. She felt the tiny spasms erupt from within. Then his other hand was between her legs, stroking her.

He stared down into her eyes.

"Look at me."

She couldn't hold his gaze. He was too beautiful, too magnificent, and had way too much power over her body. It scared her, it aroused her, and she felt her body convulse.

He did that little thing, that wasn't so little, with his fingers and she felt the jolt of her orgasm hit her hard.

She moaned and he jumped up. Grabbed onto her hands, glided his fingers between hers and stared down into her eyes.

"You are so fucking perfect." He kissed her. It was soft, then hard and arousing. He adjusted his thick, hard thighs, using them to spread her wider. The bulbous tip of his cock slid between her wet folds, as she held his gaze.

She could see him holding back. His face was tense, his eyes dark and hungry.

"I want you. Tell me you want me, too."

This was the moment of reason. "I want you, Hudson. All of you."

He tilted forward. His cock began to fill her and she tightened up, anticipating the large girth and thick muscle to tear her flesh, but Hudson paused.

"Look at me." He gripped her fingers with his tighter. He gave them a squeeze. She stared at his pectoral muscles. The lines of definition beneath the thick, hard flesh. He was a God. He was perfection.

Her eyes locked with his.

"You're mine. Every part of you is mine." He pushed into her. Taking his time, and then when she seemed to be handling the thickness and size, he eased deeper. "Just relax and let me in. We're made for one another."

Tia Rose gasped and then tried to catch her breath. He pulled back out then thrust back into her again and again. He continued to hold her gaze. She saw that he was holding back still and for her sake.

"Give me all of you, too."

His eyes widened as he pulled out and slowly pushed back into her.

"I don't want to hurt you," he whispered between clenched teeth.

"I want all of you, too, Hudson. Every inch. Take me. Make love to me…fuck me. I don't care. I just need so much. You do this to me," she whispered.

His eyes took on a look of hunger and need like she'd never seen before. He pulled his hands from her own, maneuvered his arms under her legs so they were curled over his incredibly large biceps, and spread her wide.

His initial thrust cut off her airway. She couldn't breathe. He was so big. He paused.

She shook her head. "I want it. Never like this. I feel so needy."

"God, baby, you make me crazy." He leaned forward and kissed her and then deepened his thrusts. He stroked her pussy with his cock in record speed, making her pant and moan and scratch at his skin.

"That's it, baby. Grab me. Be my wild woman." He leaned forward and licked a nipple, pulling it between his teeth and nipping her flesh. She screamed a small release as he pounded into her. The bed moaned. The cool night air circulated from the balcony and against their heated flesh.

Her moans became louder and louder as he maneuvered his one hand under her backside, and stroked a finger over the crack of her ass. She nearly shot up off the bed, but his bulk and his size kept her in place.

"Hudson."

"Come with me. Come with me now," he ordered her. She wanted to. She desperately wanted to climax along with him, but she wanted more.

"Oh, God." She clenched her teeth and then he pressed a finger against her puckered hole. He used the moisture from her sopping, wet cunt to lubricate that delicate forbidden hole then pushed in with his finger.

"Oh!" She screamed and shook. He continued to thrust into her. His face was pressed against her neck. She could feel his heavy breathing. She hugged him to her as he thrust two more times then grunted her name. Hudson rocked his hips, pulled his finger from her ass, and wrapped her in his embrace.

Rolling to his side, he took her with him and continued the onslaught of kisses, caresses, and scattered nips of gentleness.

She was breathing heavy. "Oh, my God. That was amazing."

He cupped her cheeks between his hands. He licked her lower lip and pulled it between his teeth in such a sexy, sensual move, her pussy leaked still for more.

"You're staying the night," he told her. She should argue with him. She should explain why this couldn't and shouldn't go any further than the bed and their sinful lust. But as she began to speak, her heart and her gut cut her voice off.

Live for tonight. Live for the moment. Tomorrow will come soon enough.

Chapter 5

Tia Rose awoke, hearing the sound of her cell phone chiming. Strong arms pulled her tight when she attempted to move.

She smiled wide. Hudson was holding her, and she was snuggled against him. His front was to her back, and his cock was planted between her ass cheeks and her back. She attempted to leave twice during the night. Or was it the early morning hours? She couldn't remember. They had made love several more times, and she was exhausted.

"Don't even think about leaving me yet," he whispered against her hair. His lips touched her ear, and she closed her eyes and relished in the feel of being held by him. If things were different, if her life wasn't so screwed up, she might consider getting to know him better. Scratch that. She couldn't take the chance. She couldn't wish for this to be more than a night of passion, two souls meeting in the midst of a crowded gala and falling into bed. After all, this was Paris.

"I need to get it. I should really get moving."

His forearm tightened against her belly under her breasts. He leaned up, rolled her to her back, and pressed a thigh between her legs. He was such a big man. He made her feel incredible.

"I want to spend more time with you."

She turned away a moment. "Hudson, I have things to do today. Appointments and stuff. You don't have to do this."

He gave her a squeeze and scrunched his eyebrows at her. She was getting to know that look. The man sure didn't like to be questioned or denied what he wanted. She smiled at him as if trying to ease that crease across his forehead.

"I'm not trying to make you feel wanted. I do want you. I want you to stay here. We'll have breakfast, then take a walk around. You can tell me more—"

"No." She shook her head and tried to ease up.

"I think it's better if we just keep this casual and simple, Hudson."

"Why?" he asked.

"Because it's the way it must be."

Her phone began to ring.

"I need to get that."

He sat up, rolled off the bed, and stood. The man was straight out of a history book, and appeared like some Greek God. He was solid like stone, built wide like a linebacker, but not an ounce of fat on him. He was perfection.

She began to stand up to get the phone in her purse, and as she wrapped the sheet around her body, she gasped. The sheet fell to the floor, and Hudson stood there watching her, a scowl on his face.

"Nice, Hudson," she stated, and then reached down for the sheet. He stepped on it to make it fall from her body when she got up.

"I like you naked. You're beautiful. Get back in that bed," he told her.

She raised her eyebrows at him, and of course by now she missed the call, but she was having too much fun playing with Hudson.

"Or else what?" she asked, placing her hands on her hips, and allowing the sheet to fall to the floor. There she stood in all her naked glory. Her hair probably looked a mess. Her makeup was probably smudged, and suddenly she was reaching for the sheet. Hudson had other plans.

He scooped her up into his arms and carried her back to the bed. He pressed between her thighs and cupped her breasts as he sat above her.

"You are staying a little longer."

"Really? How are you going to make me?" She felt those tiny little vibrations run rampant through her body. *The man was sexy. Oh, so very sexy.*

He pinched her nipples and she gasped as he reached up and took her hands, placing them above her head. Her breasts pushed forward, her thighs were spread wide and her pussy clenched with desire.

"I would hate to have to punish you for being naughty."

Oh boy, why did that sound so incredibly exciting? "Excuse me?" she asked.

He grabbed both wrists with one hand, securing them up and above her. He used his other hand to explore her body. As his index finger stroked over her nipple, then under the mound of her breast, he thrust his cock against her pussy. She closed her eyes and moaned. She never thought she would get turned on by being restrained, or even being spanked, but Hudson was proving to be resourceful and creative in bed.

"I always get what I want, Tia Rose. I expect you to listen to me, and allow me to bring you pleasure. I can't do that if you're not here." He pinched her nipple.

She gasped, and found herself thrusting upward against his cock. It was so close to her pussy lips, and she felt incredibly needy.

"Hudson, you can't order me to stay."

"I just did. Now here is your choice. You can be a good girl and do as I say, or, you can receive a nice spanking to teach you to obey the rules."

His words were spoken with tenacity and power. So why was she closing her eyes, and practically feeling her ass tighten?

"Tia Rose?" he wanted an answer, and when she remained silent, he made his move.

For a big guy, he was swift. He had her up, turned over on to her belly in a flash. He lifted her up and was partially over her.

When his hands caressed her ass, she suddenly wanted whatever Hudson would give her. She felt so sexy. She was completely in tune with her body. Her breasts felt full, aroused and needy. She stuck her ass back at him, dipped her hips, and closed her eyes in anticipation of his next move. She didn't care what he did, just as long as Hudson touched her and continued to arouse her so.

His fingers stroked down the crack, eliciting another soft moan.

"You like being submissive, don't you, Tia Rose?"

She shook her head.

"I think you're lying. Spread wider for me."

She immediately did.

"Good girl," he whispered and then kissed her shoulder and then her spine.

He was whispering next to her ear, as his cock tapped against her ass and pussy from behind.

"I think you would really like to get spanked. I think you would intentionally be naughty to feel my big, hard hand against this sexy, cream-colored ass."

"Oh…" she moaned and her pussy lips felt so swollen. Her cunt leaked some cream, she could feel it as she wiggled her hips.

Smack.

"Ouch."

She hadn't expected that.

"You're getting off on my words. I haven't even touched you yet."

"You just did."

Smack.

Tia Rose gasped and then pushed back.

"Are you staying or leaving?" he asked. Then he trailed his finger over her crack to her pussy. He pressed a digit up into her.

"Oh, fuck, baby, you're sopping wet."

"Do something, Hudson," she begged of him. She needed him inside of her. She ached something terrible.

"Are you staying or leaving?"

She hung her head down.

"Staying or leaving?" he asked again as he pumped his fingers faster into her pussy.

"Staying. Oh, Goddamn it, I'm staying. Now do something."

He chuckled then grabbed her hips, aligned his cock with her pussy from behind and shoved into her to the hilt.

Tia screamed his name, as she gripped the sheets, and held on for the ride.

"Oh, Hudson. Oh, my God, never felt like this. I've never allowed a man this close to me, to spank me, touch me, and say the things you've said."

Smack, smack, smack.

She gasped.

"Good. I don't want to hear about any other men touching you, spanking you, or fucking you." He thrust into her hard and she shoved back.

It suddenly turned into a challenge of who could thrust harder and deeper.

Hudson won.

She was moaning. Hudson was grunting and gripping her ass cheeks and her hips with every stroke of his cock.

Their bodies slapped together, and then he used his finger to swipe some of her cream over her anus and he pushed his finger into her forbidden hole.

Tia Rose screamed her release. Her body shook and shook until Hudson pulled his finger from her ass, smacked her ass three more times, and then grabbed her hips and held his cock inside of her. She felt the gush of hot semen flood her pussy. She relished in making him feel as wild as she felt. Tia Rose panted for breath as Hudson hugged her from behind.

He brushed the damp hair from her cheeks.

"You are perfect. And now we have more hours to play." He kissed her everywhere his mouth could reach and she lost the ability to stay upright, and fell to the bed.

He chuckled and the move parted their bodies, but she remained flat down on the bed.

Hudson massaged her ass.

"You have a beautiful ass, Tia Rose. Really beautiful." He caressed both cheeks and trailed his finger up and down the crack. She jerked and rolled to her back, pulling the covers up to cover her. But Hudson wouldn't have it.

"Come on. Let's order room service, shower, and then fool around some more. I want to take advantage of our day together."

He leaned down and kissed her, then rolled to the side of the bed and offered her his hand.

What the hell? You can only live once, Tia Rose.

She took his hand and he lifted her up and carried her across the room, stamping her heart with adoration for Hudson that would never disappear, no matter how many miles stood between them.

Chapter 6

Jagger walked into the hotel room in Paris at eleven in the evening. He was suffering from some major jet lag, and took a quick shower before getting into bed. He wasn't certain which room his brother had chosen to sleep in, but he didn't care. He was utterly exhausted.

He pulled the covers over him and he practically fell asleep the minute his head hit the pillow. He had no idea where Hudson was, but the man should be back soon. He wondered if he had remembered his surprise. He curled his lips as sleep overtook him.

* * * *

Tia Rose straightened out her dress and tried to calm her breathing. She had finally convinced Hudson to let her leave, go shower and change, and handle some business at her hotel. He said he had some things to do to, but insisted upon meeting her again. She wasn't so sure it was a good idea. He seemed so perfect, and a perfect man couldn't possibly be interested in maintaining a relationship with her. But with those negative thoughts that she knew stemmed from being hurt all her life, she remembered his actions.

The man catered to her at every moment. He doted on her every word, and actually listened to her as she spoke about her opinions on art, furniture, and today's society. He seemed to always want to be next to her, to touch her and caress her skin. That was what affected her most. Never had anyone, not even her own mother or father, give her that kind of love. But it wasn't love. This was lust, plain and simple. The sex was out of this world. She would never have sex like this again in her life, and she knew that. It was the part that sucked about leaving Hudson and Paris behind. This was a time to let loose, be free, and not worry about the consequences.

The phone calls from her father asking for money that was a day late, had really hit her hard. Hudson thought that the call she took was business related. And although he tried to pry for information, she was silent. He knew she was upset. That had led to another round of lovemaking, that time slow and deep.

She analyzed nearly every move or comment of his from yesterday. Could the man be that good of a liar? Could he really not like her body, her personality, and looks, and just be saying that he did for sex?

I love how good you feel in my arms. The way my hands look holding your ass and hips while I fuck you from behind. You have such gorgeous skin, Tia Rose, and your scent is addicting.

His words brought shivers to her body. His description of her parts, though in her eyes imperfect, made her heart swoon and her mind wander to the possibilities. But her insecurities, the lack of ever having such compliments, made her heed caution. Could he be lying?

It was quite possible. She had sex with Salvador and he basically tried to say she was beautiful and then after a month of dating, started talking to her about nutrition and diets. *Fucker!*

She did watch what she ate. It didn't matter. She was a solid woman. She had large breasts, hips, and ass, and that was it. She didn't have any flab hanging. She was tight. Salvador never made her feel anything but imperfect. Hudson made her feel gorgeous, sexy, and intoxicating. She allowed him to do things to her in one night that she never would have allowed a stranger to do. His commanding ways aroused her. To be restrained during sex had erupted something wild and rejuvenating in her. She was a new woman.

As she thought about her father's threats, and the way he called her a fat, worthless bitch, she decided to take Hudson up on his offer of meeting again tonight. Maybe she was being stupid. Perhaps she would leave Paris with a broken heart and a guilty conscious and head back to her lonely, obsolete life, but at least she had tonight. At least she could hold on to the one thing that was making her trudge onward. Hudson.

He hadn't lied to her that she knew of. He hadn't been misleading or mean to her, so she straightened out her shoulders and pulled out the hotel key card. She glanced at her watch. Eleven thirty, just as he had told her he would be back from a business meeting. He told her to wait for him if he wasn't there. He begged her to come. She was going through with this. One more night of passion, before reality arrived and she headed back to New York.

She slowly entered the hotel room. It was dark in there. She debated about turning on the lights, but decided to check to see if Hudson was in bed or not. She tiptoed toward the first room because it was closer. The other room was where they spent the last forty-eight hours. She felt her cheeks warm and her nipples harden. She had it bad. He wasn't there.

She felt disappointed and then remembered that the other room was down the hallway, where they had made love the first time.

As she entered, she saw the large bulky figure under the covers. He had fallen asleep?

She was disappointed. Why wasn't he waiting and anticipating her arrival? Or maybe he was waiting for her to make the move. First coming here alone with his key, and now, climbing into bed with him and initiating the sex.

She felt instantly nauseous, yet completely turned on. She tossed her purse onto the chair, it fell to the floor. She clenched her teeth hoping she hadn't woke him up. She would worry about finding the contents of her purse later. Right now, she needed to pretend to be an amazing seductress who was used to sneaking into sexy, hot men's hotel rooms and having her way with them.

She reached back and unzipped the dress. She hadn't bothered with a bra, and the panties were tiny and minute.

She slowly stepped out of them, and in trying to be sexy too soon, and without an audience, she nearly tumbled over. She hid her gasp, grabbed the mattress, and steadied herself. Tia Rose needed to take a few unsteady breaths. She never in her life did anything so brazen.

Holy shit. I am out of my fucking mind. I can't do this. I can't do this.

Her pussy clenched as she absorbed the site of the bulky figure under the covers. She imagined Hudson's sexy, muscles, and the warmth of his huge *embrace*. The man was a giant and that was why she fit so well beside him, and underneath him. Her pussy clenched.

I'm doing this.

Completely naked, and pussy already lubricated from this entire experience, she made her way onto the bed and under the covers.

She ran her hands along Hudson's arm, and to his chest. She slowly straddled his waist, and wished that the lights were on or at least dimmed so she could see him. But instead she felt him, and his thick long cock that began to awake. Damn Hudson felt even bigger than this morning. Could that be possible?

She heard him moan, and then whisper in a groggy voice.

"Mmm, my surprise?" he whispered.

"Oh yeah, I'm all yours," she said, and then he pulled her down to kiss him.

His kiss felt different. Not bad, but good, and he didn't hold back. He plunged his tongue deeply into her mouth and ran fingers and palms along her curves to her breasts. He immediately pinched her nipples. Hard.

She gasped, pulling from his mouth, and when she did, Hudson grabbed her by her hips, lifted her up, and pulled her forward. She had to grab onto the headboard behind him for balance, as his tongue sank into her cunt.

"Oh!" she moaned and gasped for air. He nipped at her, pulled on her clit, twirled his tongue, and then blew warm breath over her folds. As she tried to recover, she felt his fingers push into her cunt. They thrust into her, and then he curled his fingers just so, hitting some spot in her pussy that made her shoot her cream all over his face.

"Fuck yeah!" he yelled. She tensed immediately.

"Hudson?" She said his name and in an instant her body tightened. She knew that wasn't Hudson's voice.

"Fuck no, baby. I'm Jagger, and you taste fucking incredible."

She screamed as she threw herself off of him and rolled off the bed. She nearly tumbled to the floor.

She searched for her dress.

Her heart was pounding inside of her chest.

She heard another door open.

"Oh my God!" she blurted out as the lights came on and there stood Hudson in the doorway.

"What the fuck?" he yelled. She turned toward the man in the bed. The one called Jagger.

"What the hell is going on?"

She saw Hudson in the bed. But Hudson was behind her. Then she spotted the tattoos on Jagger's shoulder.

"Tia Rose?" Hudson said her name and placed his hand on her shoulder. She slapped it away.

"Get away from me. What kind of sick joke is this? I trusted you and you set me up?" She ran toward her dress, grabbed it, and shoved it on.

She felt the hand take her hand to stop her. She looked up.

Holy fucking shit. Jagger is huge and he looks pissed off.

Her pussy wept. *Jagger had a fucking talented tongue. No, I need to go. I need to get the hell out of here. They made a fool of me. Hudson was a liar, just like every other person in my life.*

"Don't go. I'm sorry. I have no fucking idea what's going on right now," Jagger said.

"What are you doing in my bed?" Hudson asked.

"I just got in about thirty minutes ago. I was fucking tired. I took a shower and got into bed. I'm suffering from some serious jet lag, bro. Then I feel this beautiful, perfect woman on top of me, and hell, I thought she was the surprise for me."

"Holy shit. Oh my God." Hudson carried on, but Tia Rose felt the tears begin to fall. She tried to grab her things and place them into her purse.

"Please, Tia. This is a complete misunderstanding," Hudson stated.

She looked up and placed her back against the wall as she slowly moved from the room.

"I trusted you, Hudson. You set this up? Is this some kind of cruel joke?" She attempted to leave. She felt so hurt and as if she were back to being the brunt of another joke.

"No. Don't go." He grabbed her hand and pulled her against his chest. He ran his hands through her hair then cupped her face between his hands.

"Don't go. This is all a misunderstanding. Please, baby, let us explain." He kissed her and she felt herself easing into his hold, but then she jerked from his mouth.

"I can't, Hudson. I just climbed into bed with your brother. I let him…he…"

"Don't go." She heard Jagger's voice. His hand moved toward her cheek and head. He cupped her cheeks and Hudson stepped slightly to the side, but remained holding her.

She looked back and forth between the identical twins. If it weren't for Jagger's tattoos, she would have a difficult time deciphering who was who.

"You're beautiful. You taste as good as you look. Stay with us."

Jagger's mouth swept down over hers and devoured her gasp. His words, his description of her taste, and the fact that he found her to be beautiful, too, made her wonder if these men were for real. This was insane.

She couldn't pull away from them. Hudson was pulling her dress slowly from her hold on it against her, and kissing her neck. "Stay. Be with us. We promise, we won't hurt you," he said.

Was he for real? Two men, gorgeous twin brothers, want me?

Jagger slowly pulled from her lips. "We'll bring you such pleasure, baby. My brother and I have particular tastes. We share everything, and I'd be honored if you'd let me bring you pleasure, too."

Holy shit. This is another major decision I'm facing. Have sex with two men I hardly know at all and fulfill a total fantasy of mine from reading so many books, or hightail it outta here and pray that I don't regret it for the rest of my life.

"Please, baby. I was going to tell you about Jagger tonight. He was supposed to be here tomorrow morning. Please, Tia Rose. Let us love you." Hudson kissed along her neck to her shoulder. Both sets of hands were pushing her dress down, and she allowed it.

"I'm going to hell, aren't I?" she asked aloud and Jagger chuckled, his warm breath colliding against her neck.

"We'll go there together, but tonight, we're doing heaven."

* * * *

Her dress fell to the floor, and Jagger lifted her up and carried her to the bed. He just earned some major points in her book. Twins. Could they be exactly alike? She didn't think so as Hudson undressed and Jagger placed her naked body down on the edge of the bed.

His cock was huge and thick. His tattoos sexy and tough.

"Your body is perfection, Tia Rose. God, I love the sound of your name. I can't wait to explore every inch of you." He leaned forward and licked the tip of her nipple. She grabbed hold of his shoulders and he cupped her breast with his other hand.

She watched him pull the tip between his front teeth, and he held it there as he stared up into her eyes.

When he closed his eyes and swirled his tongue around her nipple and areola, she closed her eyes and moaned.

She felt the bed dip, and looked up to see Hudson above her. He was holding his cock in his hands, and stroking it.

"Tia Rose, you are an amazing woman. I want you. I missed you today."

Oh, how I missed you, too.

He moved closer, leaned down, and kissed her mouth. Jagger spread her thighs wider, and then she felt his fingers press against her pussy.

"She missed you, too, bro. She's sopping wet."

She moaned when he pressed the digit up into her. Jagger seemed very gung ho.

Hudson placed a pillow under her head as he moved his cock closer.

"I want to feel your mouth on me."

She swallowed hard.

"I'm not good at it."

"I'll help you," he said.

She thought about how Salvador put her down at the way she sucked him down. He was rough, and he always shoved into her mouth when she wasn't ready. He would make her do it, and she never swallowed, no matter how hard he forced her mouth to remain on him.

"What's wrong?" Hudson asked. She shook her head. He glanced at his brother and then Jagger pulled his fingers from her cunt and leaned up and kissed her.

"Your pleasure comes first," he told her.

It was like he knew she must have had some sort of bad experience. He was thoughtful.

"Do you want to suck my brother's cock?" Jagger asked as he held her gaze. His delicious hazel eyes sparkled with mischief. Every feminine urge inside of her told her that Jagger was a very naughty man. And boy, did she want to get naughty with him. She slowly nodded her head. He was beautiful, and she probably appeared like some mute, with her mouth slightly open, drool dripping from her lips and her eyes hazed over under his spell.

"Now suck him, while I feast on your delicious pussy. I want it wet and ready for my cock."

She gasped at his words, but felt inspired to try and be sexy for him, for Hudson. She cleared her mind. Reminded herself about new beginnings and throwing the past behind her.

She stuck the tip of her tongue out to take a taste of Hudson, when Jagger, nipped her clit. She gasped and held Hudson's cock, drawing him into her mouth.

Hudson caressed her hair from her face, and then began to massage her breast. She looked up at him, their gazes locked, and she could see the intensity and need in his eyes. Jagger alternated fingers and tongue, and then he pumped his fingers into her faster. She began to suck on Hudson's cock at a similar speed. She drew him in and out with ease, and waited for him to shove into her and force her to take all of him, but it never came. Hudson continued to caress her hair, massage her breasts, and tweak her nipple. She realized that she wanted more of him. She wanted to please him and make him wild with desire. So she drew his cock into her mouth deeper, and sucked harder, as she moved her hand under his scrotum to cup his balls. The move made her pussy leak.

"Damn, baby, your mouth is sensational. I'm trying to hold back. Fuck, it feels so great. I don't want to overwhelm you, Tia."

She nodded her head, and he smiled down at her.

Hudson began to thrust a little faster into her mouth. At the same time Jagger lifted her thighs and pulled his fingers from her pussy.

"I want in, Tia Rose. Please allow me to make love to you. You got me so fucking hard, baby."

She nodded her head. She wanted him, too. She wanted to do this. As she looked at both of them. Twins, yet two different men, she felt her heart soar with excitement and hope.

Then the tip of his cock was pressing into her as Hudson cupped her face with his hands and slowly rocked into her mouth. She was doing fine. She wanted to please him, and she realized that was the difference. With Salvador she wanted to get it over with. She didn't love him. But with Hudson and Jagger, she wanted whatever they would give her. She was enjoying this.

Both men continued to thrust into her. Hudson in her mouth, moaning and whispering his pleasure, and Jagger. Jagger was definitely a man of action. He somehow hung her legs up over his upper arms to gain better access to her cunt. His thrusts were deep, and she needed to focus on Hudson's cock and pleasing him, while also maintaining her control as Jagger fucked her faster.

She felt Hudson enlarge and then he called her name. She panicked only a moment but swallowed his essence as it flowed down her throat. The moment he pulled from her mouth and fell to the side of the bed, Jagger took over.

"Arms up," he demanded as she tried to catch her breath. The taste of Hudson filled her.

"Oh God, you, too," she whispered. He gave a sly smile.

"We may be twins and do a lot of things the same, but I tend to be a bit more demanding." He thrust two quick times into her.

She stared up at him. The same hazel eyes as Hudson's, the same physique, but he had a small scar near his left eye, and he had those colorful fierce tattoos of a dragon over his shoulder and arm.

"You feel so tight, baby. My cock fits you like a glove."

"Isn't she perfect, Jagger?" Hudson asked then reached over to tweak her nipple. As she parted her lips, he took a taste of her mouth, swirled his tongue inside and then pulled out.

"I want a better look at her ass," Jagger said as he pulled out of her, making her gasp.

"On all fours. Now."

She did it immediately despite the wet, sticky feeling between her legs. She felt like a dam had broken as her cream dripped with anticipation and arousal. These men were lethal.

Smack.

She jerked forward slightly, not expecting the smack to her ass.

"She likes that a lot," Hudson said.

Before she could respond, Jagger stroked a finger in and out of her pussy from behind as he used his other hand to press her chest to the bed.

Now her ass was in his full view.

"Holy fucking shit, I've died and gone to heaven. Baby, this ass is beautiful."

"Isn't it perfect, bro? We couldn't have custom ordered this body, this woman, even if we tried," Hudson whispered as his palm slowly caressed over each globe.

"Did you fuck this perfect ass yet?" Jagger asked Hudson, and she tightened up.

Jagger chuckled.

Hudson ran a hand over her ass and squeezed her cheeks. "No. I was waiting."

"Well, the night is young," Jagger said. His words made her feel faint and excited. That was something she always wanted to try, but held off for the right man. Could she do that, too, with them? Could she give all of herself to these two men that she would leave in the morning?

Smack.

"Hey."

"I thought I was boring you," Jagger said. Hudson chuckled. But before she could reply, he thrust his cock into her pussy from behind, as he pressed a finger to her puckered hole.

Tia Rose was on fire. She thrust back and moaned at the invasion. If she died of sex, it would be worth it with these two.

* * * *

Jagger was trying not to be too rough with Tia Rose. She had come as a complete surprise to him, and apparently not the type of surprise he thought his brother was delivering. He needed to talk to Hudson and find out how he met Tia Rose. She had the perfect body, the perfect submissive reaction to them, and she was drop-dead gorgeous. He was immediately attracted to her, and he couldn't help but wonder if she were the one for them.

He pressed his finger into her ass, making her moan and shake underneath him. The sight of her ass moving as he thrust his cock into her pussy fed his ego. He wanted to mark her and claim her in every way he could. It was so strange. The possessive feeling. But as she moaned and thrust back, trying to keep up, he knew he wanted to tame her, and make her his woman their woman.

"You got me there, Tia Rose. You got me so fucking there. I want this ass. I'm going to take this ass tonight and make you mine." He pulled his finger from her ass, and wrapped an arm around her waist, hoisting her back against him. Hudson pressed his fingers to her front, and although Jagger couldn't see what Hudson was doing, he assumed that he was playing with her clit and it was working.

"Oh God, I feel something. Oh God, please, Jagger, harder, harder."

He ground his teeth and pumped his cock into her pussy, their bodies slapped together and they both moaned, as they came. He rocked his hips, bit into her shoulder, moaned, grunting, nearly feeling dizzy from his climax.

"Holy fuck," Jagger said.

Hudson cupped Tia Rose's cheeks and smiled at her, as she gasped for air.

"I know. She's amazing," Hudson said, and then kissed Tia Rose.

* * * *

I feel it in my blood. The way their hands are pressed against my skin, holding me between them. I can't believe this is happening. It's surreal. It's unbelievable. Am I dreaming? If I am, may I never awake. May my heart always feel this swollen with adoration. May my body always remember these sensations. Ultimately, may I embrace and hold on to the feelings of adequacy and perfection. Am I really so perfect in their eyes and in their embrace? Oh God, please, please don't let me screw this up. Please help me to figure out what to do. I think I love them. Oh hell, who wouldn't fall instantly in love with them? Oh, God, I can't. I can't read into this. I can't hold on to something that isn't real, isn't going to last.

Help me find a way to leave them. Help me pull away now, and take this, accept this for what it is. A night of passion. A weekend of passion in Paris with two amazing twin brothers who like to share their women. I'm one of many before me. It isn't real. This isn't something to last. It's a sexual encounter. It's over. It can't go on. Leave now. Leave before I cry. Leave now. Leave now.

She stirred the moment the fingers pressed against her nipple, and then the hand cupped her breast. She wouldn't open her eyes. She wanted to memorize their touch. It would be the one thing that would help her sleep at night, and recall their attention to her.

"Your skin is so silky smooth and your hair. It smells incredible." Jagger said then sniffed her hair, while he tortured her resolve. A caress, a pinch and a twist, and her pussy leaked with need.

She opened her eyes as Hudson maneuvered between her thighs.

"Good morning, princess."

His words and his nickname stirred sadness in her heart and also pleasure. Surely as a child in her family, she was not a princess but a burden, a displeasure, and a punching bag. Now, between these two worldly amazing men, she was far from a princess. She was a temporary lover, a ship passing in the night. There was no need for pet names, or anything else to bind them. She gave a small smile.

"What is it? What's wrong?" Hudson asked, but Jagger also took on the same concerned expression as his brother. She stared up at both identical twins and her heart ached something terrible.

Leave them now. It will only get worse if you wait.

"I have to get going."

"No." They both responded so fast, and held her tightly. They shocked her.

"I have to. You know I do, Hudson. I'm leaving Paris soon, and I have things to do for work," she lied. She had no more work to do. The last bit of pictures and drawings she had finished yesterday to help pass the time and keep her mind off of last night and coming to Hudson's hotel room. Boy, had so much changed in the last few hours.

"What kind of work do you do?" Jagger asked. She tilted her head at him sideways and gave a small, knowing smile. The small talk wouldn't keep her there longer. Plus, she wasn't giving them more information on her.

"I had a wonderful time. I'm so glad that I met you both. You've made this first trip to Paris so memorable. But reality is rearing its ugly head."

Jagger and Hudson both looked upset, but Jagger seemed downright pissed off.

"I want to know how to contact you."

She shook her head.

"Why not?"

"What for? I know what this is. You explained about how you share women. I understand the deal, and I accepted it last night. Please. Just let me go."

They could hear a cell phone ringing.

"That's mine. I need to get that."

Tia Rose got up from the bed and grabbed her dress to cover herself up. She noticed her purse and the items scattered on the rug. She remembered dropping it last night as she had the shock of her life. She saw the light and the phone and grabbed it. Anything to pull away from a dramatic exit from the twins.

"Hello."

She walked out of the bedroom and into the bathroom.

"Miss Richman?"

"Yes," she replied, not recognizing the voice.

"My name is Detective Ovens. I'm calling from the 46th Precinct in New York. I was wondering if you could tell me where your brother, Sean, is. Have you heard from him?"

"What? My brother, Sean? No. Why? What happened?"

"He's wanted for questioning in an armed robbery in Missouri."

"Oh, my God. Are you serious?"

"Yes, ma'am. If you're helping him, I need to know. I need you to turn him in."

"Oh, I can assure you that I'm not helping him, Detective Ovens. First of all, I'm in Paris right now on business, and secondly, I haven't spoken to my brother in five years."

"I spoke with your parents. They weren't very cooperative."

"They're not nice people, Detective."

"You've been sending them money."

"How do you know that?"

"It's my job to know. It seems that your brother headed here to New York. I'm working with other investigators. When are you returning to the city?"

"Tomorrow. Late evening."

"Can I leave you my number for you to call me?"

She looked around the bathroom.

"I don't have a pen. Can you text me the number? I don't think there's anything more I can help you with though."

"I'll determine that when we meet. You're sure that he wouldn't come to see you? Maybe try to get money from you?"

"No. He hates me."

"Those are harsh words."

"His treatment was harsher. I'm sorry, but I can't help you."

She disconnected the call then felt her gut clench and her heart race. She needed to get home. The perfect wonderful time with Hudson and Jagger was over. Reality came crashing back. Now here she was again, trying to separate herself from a family with bad intentions, and specifically, a brother wanted by the law. How was this going to affect her life? Could he cause her trouble? Could he actually try to contact her for help? She could lose her job. She could go to jail for aiding and abetting, even though she did no such thing. *Oh, my God, my life will never improve. They'll always have control of me. They'll always bring me down.*

The knock on the door frightened her.

"I'll be right out," she said, and then threw the dress over her head, zipped up the back best she could, and ran her fingers through her hair. She saw the tube of toothpaste on the counter and quickly spread some onto her finger as a makeshift toothbrush. She rubbed it in then spit it out, nearly gagging.

She fixed herself best she could, adjusted her boobs into the tight bodice, and took a deep breath.

Back to reality.

* * * *

"Is everything okay?" Hudson asked as Tia Rose emerged from the bathroom. She was dressed and she looked like an angel.

"Yes. I need to go. Something came up."

Jagger grabbed her hand and pulled her against his chest. He was staring down into her eyes. She had no shoes on and she looked so petite and feminine.

"Tell me there's not another man."

"Please, Jagger. I need to go. This is over."

He covered her mouth and kissed her deeply. Hudson felt his cock grow hard just watching. They were good together. Scratch that, they were perfect. What could he do to get her to stay or at least get her tell them how to contact her?

Jagger released her lips and hugged her.

"Can I give you our card? Maybe think about calling us?" he asked.

He pulled it out and placed it into her hand as she shook her head, no.

Hudson pulled her into his arms next.

He stared down into her gorgeous green eyes. His gut clenched. He was overwhelmed with a feeling of possessiveness and regret.

"Tell me you'll call us."

"Please, Hudson. Don't make this more difficult than it is. It's better this way. I need to go."

She was pulling from his arms, and he pulled her back and kissed her deeply. When he finally let her go, he could see the tears in her eyes, and her cell phone was ringing again.

Was she involved with someone else? He never asked her. She asked him, and of course, he told her no. They stood there and watched her leave. As the door closed, Jagger shook his head.

"She was fucking perfect, Hudson. Perfect."

"I know. But we can't force her to stay, to tell us who she really is, and where she lives."

Jagger ran his hands through his hair then walked toward the bed. He pulled on his jeans and then stopped.

"You don't have any idea where she lives?"

Hudson shook his head. He was angry. He should try to stop her again, but then she may get scared. He didn't want to scare her. Something in her eyes told him she was untrusting and that this whole weekend was not a normal thing for her. God, he hoped it wasn't. He didn't want to think about her with someone else.

"Hey, is this yours?" Jagger asked, holding out a small piece of paper.

"What is it?" Hudson took it and looked at it.

"A piece of a receipt of some kind. For a money transfer."

"No. It's not mine. It says to Missouri. Of course the name of the sender's missing."

"Maybe it's Tia Rose's. Maybe that's where she's from?"

Hudson felt the excitement and then the need to respect her wishes.

"I don't think she's from there. We can't do anything about it. She made her decision. She left us. It's over. I'm going to go shower."

Hudson left the room, and as he started the shower and grabbed the soap, he closed his eyes and envisioned her. She had been the most beautiful woman he had ever met. How could he let her go? How could he have been so stupid to have not asked her more questions?

Because I fear opening up my heart to any woman. None of them can be trusted. None had proven they wanted his love or his heart, only his money.

Chapter 7

"You worthless bitch! Where's the money?" her father screamed at her over the telephone. She was at work and trying to get over the fact that someone broke into her apartment. The police thought that it may have been her brother, but the small safe she had bolted down in her closet wasn't even tampered with. Instead, her lingerie, her entire bedroom, including her drawing desk, computer and supplies were.

"I sent you the thousand dollars."

"Bullshit! You're holding out. Now you don't want to pay us? You think you're too good. We took care of you. You owe us for putting up with your fat, disgusting self."

The tears stung her eyes. When were her parents name-calling and insults going to not affect her? When?

"It can't be. I did send it. I have five thousand dollars in that account."

"Five thousand and you only send us one? If you were here right now, Tia, I'd give you an ass whipping and you'd be damn sure to show me respect. Send us the money and make it two thousand from now on."

He hung up the phone. His voice and his threats lingered in her mind. She tried to stop the shaking. She was almost as upset as when the detectives asked her if she had an ex-boyfriend or lover who was stalking her. Maybe someone she met that didn't want her out of his life. She mentioned Salvador. She had thought about Hudson and Jagger. No way. They weren't those kind of men. But she did have to ask herself the question, which only led to her missing them, and the safety of their arms. She made her decision. Now she had to live with it.

Her father frightened her even more so than her brother.

She pulled her personal account information up on the bank computer. She then saw that her savings account was still secure, and her mere twenty-two thousand dollars and twenty cents were still there. She sighed in relief. Not that it was much, but it was hers.

She then opened up the small account she set up to do direct money transfers to Western Union through her account to her parents' account. As she logged in and saw the balance, she was shocked. It was at zero. Three phone calls later and then one to the police, she realized she had been robbed. Detective Owens said that if it were her brother or someone else who ransacked her apartment and took any leftover receipts that they could then steal the money from the account.

The bank was trying to trace the money, but it was a Saturday, and the bank would be closing soon. Monday could give more answers.

She then had to withdraw a thousand dollars, not two, from her savings to a new direct transfer account. She refused to send the man two thousand dollars. She just couldn't survive if she kept that up once a month. That was like a house mortgage.

At least work was going well. She had impressed the board with her new ideas, and was finalizing the fall catalogue for publishing. She was finally where she belonged and getting the recognition she felt she deserved. But even now, with her work a success, she had an even greater hollow feeling inside.

She wished she could have stayed in Paris with Hudson and Jagger forever.

* * * *

"Okay, so let me get this straight. Hudson, you meet this sexy, full-figured goddess, the answer to your fantasies, in Paris and sleep with her. Then, while you're running late from a meeting, Jagger is asleep in the hotel room with jet lag, and this woman mistakes him for you?" Jett asked.

"Then Jagger has his way with her until she realizes it's not Hudson. So even after all the confusion, she stays with the two of you, and now you want us to help you two find her?" Flynn asked.

Zane, Cash, Nash, and Riker sat around the poker table half shocked and half chuckling. Emerson and Stone were smiling ear to ear.

"Ahh, so now that the two of you found an amazing woman, it's not so corny to feel in love?" Stone asked with an attitude.

Hudson knew that he and Jagger had teased the guys immensely when they met their women, but he was too on edge right now to fight with them.

"Fuck you. This is crazy. We met her, she's perfect, but she seemed scared."

"Well, hell, Hudson, look at the size of you and your fucking brother. People move out of the way the moment you enter a room. You probably scared her, double-teaming her like that," Stone teased.

"Stop being such a dick," Jagger replied.

"Well, what do you know about her?" Flynn asked.

"What made you think that she was scared?" Cash asked.

"She got this phone call when she was going to leave. She seemed really shaken up and just scared. It was a gut instinct, but I think she was in trouble or it was bad news," Hudson replied.

"We don't know where she lives. We did find this Western Union money transfer receipt in the hotel room. It was half ripped, so we couldn't get her name, just that the money went to Missouri," Jagger added.

"Was the whole account number on there?" Jett asked as he rose from his seat.

"Only part of it," Hudson said.

"Well, if you have it, give it to me and I'll see what I can come up with," Zane offered.

"You'd do that?"

"Shit, Hudson, I'm sitting here half in shock that the two of you found a woman you both want and are this dead set on finding her. Didn't anyone even ask where she was from?"

"She didn't want to exchange information," Hudson said then ran his hand through his hair. He was still kicking himself in the ass for not asking questions. If he had, she would be with them right now.

Two weeks had passed and still, neither he nor Jagger could get Tia Rose out of their head.

"Did you get her name at least?" Cash asked.

"Tia Rose."

Emerson whistled. "That's sweet."

"I know," Jagger said with eyebrows raised.

"You two really want to find this woman from Paris?" Emerson asked.

Hudson looked at Jagger. They had been talking nonstop about her for days now. It was starting to piss them off.

"Yes," they both replied, and their friends chuckled.

"I love that simultaneous twin shit," Stone remarked.

"We'll help you. We'll get started on it after the game. Come on and let's enjoy our poker night," Jett stated.

"Yeah, until these guys' girlfriends call them on their curfew," Flynn teased the others.

"You wish you had a woman like Chastity to go home to," Riker replied as he dealt the cards out.

"Or a woman like Chiara. She'd mess your shit up, Flynn," Zane added.

"I'd be careful what you say about Toni, Jett and Flynn. She won't be special delivering any of those raspberry brownie bites you've both learned to love so much," Stone added then smiled.

"Whatever," Jett said.

Hudson had to laugh at the scowl on his and Flynn's faces. Those two would never settle down. It would take one hell of a woman, and they were too blind to realize.

Hudson just hoped they could help them find Tia Rose. When they did, he and Jagger would make her see that what they had was real, and they were fortunate enough to meet in France to share the best weekend of all their lives.

* * * *

Jagger was standing in the study of their penthouse thinking about Tia Rose. He had never been infatuated with anything in his life, never mind a person. He came from a broken family. He and Hudson had to build their own lives and keep the negativity behind them. Their father left them as soon as he realized what having a family and a wife were all about. He wanted to party, to drink, and to do drugs, which ultimately killed him. Not having a father made times tough. But together he and Hudson survived.

Their mom was a single mom, who worked two jobs to help pay for their college education. She had struggled her entire life, until she met Richey and Daniel. Now they were living life on a yacht, currently somewhere in the Caribbean.

"Hey, what's that smirk about?" Hudson asked, as he entered the room with Jett and Flynn.

Jagger straightened out and gave his firm, serious, and usual expression. Hudson squinted his eyes but Jett and Flynn couldn't resist teasing.

"Thinking about your Tia Rose?" Jett asked.

Jagger shook his head, and then joined them by the couches.

"No, I was actually thinking about Mom, Rich, and Daniel. Wondering where they're headed next."

"Shoot, they haven't called in two weeks. Maybe we should check on Mom," Hudson said, looking concerned.

"I am sure that Melody is safe and secure with her two retired Marines," Flynn replied.

He was right. Daniel and Richie, though in their fifties, were more than capable of handling security and safety for Jagger and Hudson's mom, Melody.

"So, what's this visit about?" Jagger asked.

"Oh, Cash and Zane are on their way over," Hudson announced.

"Chiara is coming with them," Flynn teased.

"Hey, she's not pissed at me anymore for hitting on her at the club. I was just trying to get Cash and Zane fired up. Besides, that was months ago," Jagger added, and they just chuckled. The doorbell sounded and Hudson went to answer it. A few seconds later along came Cash, Zane, and Chiara, looking as beautiful as ever. Of course Zane kept his arm wrapped around her midsection. Both Cash and Zane adored her. They nearly lost her, so it was understandable.

"Hello, Chiara, come on in. Can I get you anything to drink? Or something else?" Jagger teased.

She blushed and Cash gave Jagger a look.

"Don't try to cause any trouble. Your wise guy games won't work on us a second time," Zane added.

"Yeah, well, the one time it was pretty freaking funny."

"Now, now, boys, there's no need for an argument. God knows we've been over that incident way too many times. Ouch," Chiara squealed as Zane gave her a light smack on her backside. She gave him an angry look. He held his ground and she placed her hands on her hips then moved next to him. It was a sight to see. They adored her and Chiara adored Cash and Zane. He wanted that. Those small glances that meant so much. He never had that.

"So, we brought Chiara along because we found out some information on your missing French goddess," Cash stated, then walked closer to them and handed over a file to Hudson and Jagger.

Jagger swallowed hard and looked at Hudson, who was just as nervous. "Good news or bad news?" Hudson asked as they opened up the file.

There was a copy of Tia Rose's driver's license, picture included.

"Is this in the city? Here in New York?" Hudson asked as Jagger thought the same thing.

"It is. She lives in New York and works not far from here," Cash told them.

"Holy shit. Where? What's the name of the place?" Hudson asked.

"Okay, this is where it gets down to the, unfortunately, tricky part in sharing our information. First of all, what are you going to do when you find her?" Cash asked.

"What the fuck do you mean? We're going to talk to her, get things going, so we can learn more about her," Hudson stated.

"She's in a bit of a situation right now," Zane told them.

"What kind of situation?" Hudson asked, before Jagger could.

"I spoke with a friend of mine on the force. Seems her apartment had been broken into and ransacked. No money was taken and the safe she had was secured, but lingerie and other work-related items were destroyed," Cash stated.

"Who did it?"

"That's the other thing. It seems her brother from Missouri might have been involved in an armed robbery and then headed to New York, maybe to get cash from her," Zane said.

"Shit. Is she close to him?" Hudson asked.

"Will she be charged with aiding and abetting?" Jagger asked.

"She's not close with him or her parents, yet she sends them money every month," Zane said.

"The receipt from the Western Union was from Tia?" Jagger asked, and Cash nodded his head.

"It seems that she left home five years ago, and has been taking care of herself since," Zane said.

"Tell them about what Dante Perrone told Jett," Chiara said.

"What?" Hudson asked.

Jagger thought the guys seemed a bit uncertain of whether they should tell them.

"What did Dante say? How is he involved?" Jagger asked them.

"Dante has done business with the firm Tia works at. He said before she left Paris, she had been in a bad state and had been really down. He knows one of the secretaries, Alexa, that works there. Alexa told him that Tia never talked about her family, and is always alone. She was dating some older guy, but then it stopped. Dante said that since returning she looks great, her attitude has changed, and she finally stood up for herself against one of the bosses who was stealing her designs."

"Stealing her designs? Tia is a designer? Of what?"

Jett smiled.

"Everything you're looking for in a home decorator, bud. She designs furniture and produces a catalog for Malone's," Chiara told them.

"Wow. I like that company. It's not high end, but it's nice. I think Dante just sent me the catalog for September this morning," Hudson said, and then stopped and looked at them. "That fucker knew. Unbelievable."

"Well, don't get upset with him. He has a plan for the two of you to meet Tia, so you don't spook her," Jett said.

"Spook her?"

"Yep, he thinks she's perfect for the two of you. So call him," Jett stated and then stood up.

"Holy crap. But what about all this other stuff?" Jagger asked them.

"We could find out everything if you need. I mean her bank account, her social security number, any arrests, as well as ex-boyfriends if you want. We can even find out why she left home and why she keeps sending money to people who don't call her except once a month around the time the money gets sent to Missouri," Cash added as he stood up as well.

Jagger understood it. They didn't want to pry too much.

"Hey, we appreciate that. We asked for you guys to help us find her and you did. We'll take the next steps now," Jagger said.

"Call Dante. His plan sounds so good," Chiara said as they kissed her good-bye and then shook their friends' hands good-bye.

"We will. Thanks."

As everyone left, Hudson walked back toward the living room. Jagger was staring at her picture.

"She's so beautiful, Hudson. But my gut is clenched with concern. I think there's more to this break-in and this whole sending money to her parents."

"Well, I sure as shit would hope you weren't blind to that. I feel it, too. She needs us and we need her. Call Dante."

"Okay. I will, and you check out this catalog. I bet we can get her to accompany us to the country home and start remodeling there. Three weeks in our arms should do the trick," Jagger said, passing the magazine to Hudson.

Hudson chuckled. "That might work out just fine." He leaned back with the catalog in hand.

Jagger hoped that this was the beginning of getting their woman back into their arms where she belonged and where they needed her to be.

* * * *

There was a knock at her office door and Alexa came in.

"Hey, Dante Perrone is on line one. He's asking to speak with you."

"Me? I just saw him yesterday."

"I know," Alexa said then raised her eyebrows up and down.

Tia Rose answered the phone wondering what the man wanted. It was funny, but since she returned from Paris, she had gotten so many compliments about her style, her hair, and her body. It was still the same size-twelve body, but she learned how to accentuate the better parts and draw focus to her eyes and face with the right application of makeup. She felt really good about herself, but now she was nervous as she spoke with Dante. They exchanged pleasantries and he asked about France. He named some places he loved to dine out at and she wasn't impressed in the least. She could care less about his money, and mostly about him continuing to use Malone's for all his high-end store decorating.

"So, I have a proposition for you. Well, actually, I would like for you to accompany me to dinner this evening."

She gulped. Dante Perrone was asking her out?

"Um, I don't think that's such a good idea."

"Nonsense. You are a very attractive woman. I need you tonight. You see, I have a friend who is in need of a personal designer. He hasn't had much success with the local area stores or abroad. Anyway, I told him all about you, and I was wondering if you could assist him. Perhaps give him some ideas this weekend at his estate?"

"I'm not too sure if I'm interested. I never really did that before. I have a lot to do with cleaning up the apartment after the break-in."

"Oh, yes, that's right. What a terrible way to return home after such a worthwhile trip to Paris. Well, I think you'll change your mind the moment you meet the potential client. I planned a meeting at LaFonte's tonight. My treat, of course. Can you be there by seven?"

She didn't want to, but she felt that if she didn't, she could upset Dante, and he was a good client of Malone's.

"Okay. I'll meet you there."

She continued to chat for a few more seconds and then he ended the call. Now she would have to find something to wear. Perhaps one of the casual yet stylish designer black dinner dresses she found in a boutique near Versailles?

She went back to work, and began to wonder if perhaps this could lead to other opportunities, and some extra income. If she was going to continue to care for her unappreciative family, she needed more money.

She pondered over her own thought. *Why do I continue to let my parents control me like this? They don't love me. They never did.*

What she really needed was a therapist. They'd have a field day with her. She just couldn't let go. She couldn't cut ties, no matter how bad her mother and father treated her, because they were her parents. It wasn't right. She wanted to please them, but maybe she never would be able to, no matter what their demands.

Even asking her to die would be unlikely to please them. That would make them have to work for a living, instead of live off her hard-earned money. With aggravating thoughts, Tia Rose headed back to work on her computer.

Chapter 8

"She's late. She's not coming, Hudson. She figured it out," Jagger stated as he and his brother stood by the side of the building. They were watching the front entrance to the restaurant, waiting to arrive for the dinner meeting that Dante arranged.

"She'll be here. She always works late at Malone's. She had to go home, change, and then take local transportation to get back across town to here," Hudson replied.

"Yeah, well, as soon as she's our woman, she's moving in with us. I don't want her living in that neighborhood. There's no security there. No wonder her apartment was broken into."

Hudson looked back at his brother.

"Jagger, you can't be so pushy. Not right off the bat, anyway. You'll scare Tia Rose. Promise me that you won't go all cave man on her."

Jagger looked away. He was biting the inside of his cheeks. He couldn't believe he was standing outside of a fucking restaurant like some damn stalker waiting for their lover to arrive. This was fucking ridiculous. When he wanted something, he went after it and took it. No bullshit. He felt as if he were walking on eggshells and any wrong move could send Tia Rose out of their lives. Again. He couldn't let that happen.

Hudson bumped his shoulder.

"Fine. I promise. But not for the entire night. I'm a no-bullshit guy. You fucking know that. If there needs to be a calm, rational one, then you be that person. I don't have the patience." He glanced at his watch for the tenth time in the last thirty minutes. "Where the fuck is she?"

* * * *

Tia Rose was still shaking. She almost cancelled this dinner date, but her gut told her not to. She wasn't going to live in fear. When she arrived at her apartment, she felt uneasy. Like someone had been in there again. The detectives working the break-in at her place as well as the investigation and pursuit of her brother Sean said that her feelings were normal. Violated? She sure as shit felt violated. It took her hours to fall asleep and she was debating about taking some sleeping pills but worried that if someone broke in, they could rob her, rape her, and possibly kill her while she was dead to the world.

As she had entered her apartment tonight, she had a strong sense of creepiness. Something was bugging her out. Even tonight as she left her apartment, and traveled across town to meet Dante, she felt as if someone was watching her. She kept glancing over her shoulder. Living in New York over the last five years taught her to be aware of her surroundings and to walk with purpose and direction even if she were lost. She supposed it was like this in all big cities, but she especially felt vulnerable. There was no one to walk with. No one to make her feel safe. She was all alone, and that was what her future held. Sometimes she debated about returning to Missouri, because even painful attention was better than no attention at all.

Felling sorry for herself, she exited the commuter bus, two blocks from the restaurant. She cringed just thinking about the trip back to her apartment late tonight. *Why did I agree to this?*

Because you always do as you're asked. Dante is a nice person, and he could be hooking me up with some serious side money. Money I'll need to keep supporting my screwed-up parents.

She took a deep breath and straightened out her skirt before she entered the restaurant. The host immediately smiled at her upon her arrival, as he looked her over. "Good evening, miss. Table for one?" he asked.

"No, I'm meeting someone. Mr. Perrone."

His smile faded only momentarily. She wondered if perhaps he knew Dante and didn't care for him. She felt like confronting the man, feeling some loyalty toward Dante, and how nice he had always been to her over the past year.

"Lucky man. Follow me please, miss," he said, and she understood now. Her cheeks warmed. The host had found her attractive and was disappointed knowing she was meeting a man. How funny. She admired the host's good looks and was about to say that she was only friends with Dante, when she spotted the private table, way in the back and secluded from the rest of the restaurant. She could hardly see where he was sitting as the booth curved just so, and blocked anyone's view from the seats and table within. Very private. Her belly tightened.

What exactly did Dante have in mind? She felt her belly flutter with concern. Every time she thought about accepting a date from new admirers, she thought of Hudson and Jagger, and her heart ached. Her affair in Paris had ruined her for any other man. She was really one fucked-up individual.

"There you are. I was getting worried," Dante said as he leaned forward and kissed her cheek. He looked at her dress as he smiled.

"You, look, gorgeous!" He spoke the words slowly and with gusto. She smiled at him. The man looked very good, too. But that was Dante. Suit, tux, casual wear, it didn't matter. He was a model.

"Thank you. You look wonderful, too. So how did you get so lucky to get this table?" she asked, as he motioned with his hand for her to take a seat in the booth.

"Oh, I have my connections. So, is everything okay? You're usually so punctual."

"I'm sorry. It's just that since my apartment was broken into, I feel so violated and nervous when I go home and when I leave there. I know it's normal, but it's taking a toll on me."

"Well, that's understandable. Perhaps you won't be going home alone this evening." She felt her cheeks warm and an uneasy feeling hit her gut. Was he suggesting that he would be in her bed tonight?

"Dante, I don't think that—"

He placed his finger up in the air for her to stop talking. "Your potential clients have arrived. Remember, destiny is what you make of it, Tia Rose. Anything is possible when you follow your heart and your gut."

What?

She turned to see what or whom had made Dante speak in such a way. She instantly felt nervous, unsure, and utterly confused. And then they were there. Standing in front of the table. Six feet four and larger than life, Hudson and Jagger.

"Good evening, my goddess," Jagger stated.

"Tia Rose, finding you has been quite the challenge," Hudson added.

Her throat closed up. The tears filled her eyes. She felt sick to her stomach, excited, scared, and utterly shocked as she covered her mouth with her hand.

A glance toward Dante and he smiled.

"Your destiny. Everything happens for a reason, Tia Rose. Enjoy the evening, and let me know how working for Jagger and Hudson Ross, decorating their vacation home works out for you."

She watched Dante walk away.

"How? What is going on?" she began to say when Hudson took her hand and pulled her up.

"Come to me, baby. God, we've missed you," he said as she slid closer to the edge, allowing the large, thick hand of his to take her smaller hand, and pull her up. The instant he touched her, she laid her head against his solid chest and inhaled his cologne. Then she cried.

"Oh, God, Hudson, I've missed you both so much. How did you find me? How do you know Dante?" She wiped the tears.

He cupped her cheeks and stared down into her eyes. "We had to find you. You're our woman and we need you. Life just isn't the same without you." He leaned down and kissed her softly on the lips, then hugged her tight.

She was shaking as he smiled then released her to Jagger. Jagger pulled her against his chest and held her cheek with the palm of his hand as his other hand plastered over her ass. Exactly where she loved it.

"You were difficult to find, but now that we're back together, we're not letting you go."

Before she could react, he kissed her as Hudson chuckled behind her. She felt his chest against her back, and she was instantly safe and secure. She felt complete between them as she kissed Jagger back until he slowly released her lips.

"We have two choices. One, we stay here eat and then head back to our place. Or two, we skip dinner and we have you instead."

She chuckled. "I think we should talk first. This is a shock to me."

He smiled. "Okay, but after we talk, I want you. In my bed, under me, with my cock buried deep in your wet pussy and Hudson's cock buried deep in your ass. Between us, part of us, is where you belong."

Oh, my God. This is crazy.

She closed her eyes and took a shaky breath.

"Jagger, I said to go slowly and don't scare the woman. Let's sit down, order some drinks and food, and talk," Hudson said, and she nearly fell into the seat. Her legs were shaking, but her body was ready to be taken by Hudson and Jagger.

* * * *

Hudson couldn't stop touching Tia Rose, and neither could Jagger. They sat beside her, caressed her hands, her thighs beneath the table, as they ate, drank, and talked about whom they really were.

"I can't believe that you both live here in New York, too. Where exactly?" she asked as she took a sip of wine. Hudson watched her mouth sip at the glass, and then she lowered the glass and licked her lips as she looked back and forth between them.

"Manhattan. In a penthouse on Fifth Avenue," Jagger whispered and then leaned closer, gently moving her hair away from her ear and cheek, so he could kiss her skin.

"You smell so good. Exactly as I remember."

"Oh, God, what did you say that the two of you do?"

Hudson smiled, as he repeated Jagger's move on her left side, as he kissed her ear and whispered.

"We're entrepreneurs." He hid his chuckle as he felt her shaking, and from his view above her, he could tell her nipples hardened through the form fitted dress she wore.

"Fifth Avenue is very expensive. Like millions of dollars a year for a penthouse. Um, what exactly are you two telling me?"

"You're very smart," Jagger stated, still kissing her neck.

"And very beautiful," Hudson added, kissing her other side.

"I'm about to have a panic attack." She held on to the table. Both of them moved away, and covered each of her hands with theirs.

"Just relax. It doesn't matter that we're billionaires."

She jerked up toward Hudson. Her eyes were as wide as saucers and he had to laugh. "This isn't funny. This is not happening. You two can have any woman you want. Hell, you could order the perfect woman from a goddamn menu. Why are you here with me?"

Jagger moved quicker than Hudson could as her words shocked him.

He turned her face toward him. Jagger cupped her cheeks and stared down into her eyes.

"You are fucking perfect for us. You're better than anything anyone could pull off a menu, baby. We want you. We want this body. We want you in our arms every fucking day and night. You're gorgeous, sexy, and everything we've ever wanted." He kissed her hard on the mouth, and she held on to his forearms, kissing him back. When he released her lips, they were both panting.

"You're not playing a game with me?" she asked, and Hudson could tell that she was serious. He wondered who had hurt her so badly that she couldn't trust or believe them.

"Never, baby. Never," Jagger said. Hudson placed his hands on her shoulders. He whispered next to her ear.

"We want you. We searched for you because we missed you that much."

"We even got our friends involved, and thank God we've known Dante for years. When we found out that you were here in New York, we were thrilled," Jagger told her.

"This is too much. I feel so confused," she whispered.

"Honey, you're coming home with us tonight. We're going to spend the weekend together, and then we're going to make some definite plans," Jagger stated.

"Wait. I don't want to be just some sex toy."

Hudson chuckled. "Hell, woman, you are way more than that."

"Wait, why do you want to be with me?" She was amazing. She really didn't know why they wanted her.

"Because you're meant to be ours. That weekend in Paris was the best weekend of our entire lives. I know that you're scared and untrusting. We'll get to why you're so untrusting and insecure later. Right now you need to know that we're for real. We want you in our lives."

"In our bed," Jagger said.

"Come home with us tonight. Let's spend the weekend talking and working things out."

"Making love and us learning every inch of this luscious body."

She chuckled. "You're crazy."

"About you," Jagger said and kissed the corner of her mouth. She lowered her eyes. Hudson placed his fingers under her chin so that she would look up at him.

"Crazy about you. Take this chance. Again. Be with us. Let's see where it leads."

She was silent, and his gut clenched with worry that she would say no, and leave them again. He didn't want that. He couldn't handle that.

"Okay," she whispered.

He smiled as Jagger raised his hand and called out, "Check." Tia Rose giggled, and the sound grabbed a hold of his heart and latched on forever.

* * * *

Who was she with now? Was she some kind of whore? I thought tonight would be the perfect night, but it seems I can cause you more pain, Tia, if I wait to strike. I've enjoyed this time. Waiting, planning. I've been quiet for the most part, and especially when it came to you. I don't want to wait. I want to cause you pain. I want to hear you beg for help, plead to the darkness of the night. You deserve to be alone. Alone and dead. I'm ready to send you there. Oh, am I so ready to send you to your grave, bitch.

I'll get you soon. When you're all alone, in that shitty little apartment you call a home, maybe even while you're sleeping in that dinky twin-sized bed made for a child, not a fat, ugly woman like you. I can't wait to see your face. To know that it's me who takes your last breath away. Soon. I need this. I want this. I will kill you.

Chapter 9

Tia Rose was literally shaking as they entered the penthouse suite. From the time Hudson pulled the Audi up front for the valet to take the car and the doorman to greet them, she felt out of sorts. It was like she was having an out-of-body experience. The fanfare they received upon entering had her feeling completely out of her league. Women looked Hudson and Jagger over with hungry eyes, and then toward her with daggers.

Even the elevator escort seemed surprised that the men were bringing her up to their home. She felt that bit of lack of self-confidence. Her inadequacies were glowing like a neon sign for all to see.

"Hey, are you okay?" Hudson asked, cupping her chin and tilting it up toward him.

My God, he's so beautiful and big. He's perfection and I'm not. They probably bring models and sexy women up here all the time. My God, what am I thinking?

"Tell me what crazy thoughts are running through your head," Hudson said, giving her chin a light squeeze.

"I'm thinking about how many women you two bring up to your penthouse, as you parade them through the lobby, as all the other women gawk and drool."

He stared at her and shook his head tsk-tsking a moment. He held her gaze.

"Jameson, please tell Miss Richman how many women my brother and I bring up to our penthouse." She assumed that he meant the escort.

Jagger spoke up.

"Look her in the eyes. Our woman has some trust issues we need to work out."

She swallowed hard as Jagger rubbed his hands together. Why did she think his idea of working out her trust issues meant his hand across her backside giving her a spanking? She nearly moaned, her body was so turned on at the thought.

She felt her cheeks blush, and six feet four Hudson remained staring at her, holding her chin firmly.

"Miss Richman, I have operated this elevator for the last twenty years. I know everything that goes on. I can tell you in complete honesty that Mr. and Mr. Ross have never brought a woman up to their penthouse. This is their home. Even I am shocked that you are here with them," he told her.

She swallowed hard.

As the elevator stopped, the doorman waited as Jagger pressed a code in the panel. Then the doors opened. Tia Rose was pleasantly stunned at the gorgeous, wide entryway, and could already tell that these men had class and style.

"Thank you, Jameson," Jagger said.

Tia Rose turned to look at the elevator man.

"Thank you, Jameson."

"My pleasure, miss. Good night," he said, and the doors closed.

Hudson took her hand and led her inside. "I don't want to waste time giving you the tour right now. We need you, Tia Rose." He wrapped his arms around her waist and pulled her against him. "Kiss me and take us to bed," he told her, and she giggled.

He was so damn charming and sexy. Every time she thought she had him identified, he did something else to surprise her. Reaching up and wrapping her arms as best she could around his shoulders considering how tall he was, she smiled. "With pleasure, Hudson."

He lowered his mouth, and she quickly closed the space between them and kissed him.

* * * *

Jagger quickly undressed as Hudson carried Tia Rose to their bedroom. She was kissing him, and Hudson surprisingly hadn't tripped along the way. She looked so good. His dick was so hard he couldn't wait to make his words to her from back in the restaurant a reality.

Hudson set her feel gently down onto the rug. He moved around her and began to undo the zipper of her dress. Her swollen, well-kissed lips were parted as the dress fell from her luscious body.

Jagger caressed a finger along her breasts, down the slight swell of her belly to her pussy. "Strip, then get over here, like I told you back at the restaurant."

She looked about shocked, but highly aroused, as Hudson unclipped her bra, and it fell from her body. His cock grew, so did his eyes. She was luscious. Her nipples were hard, her areolas full and waiting for his mouth.

He licked his lips as he stroked his cock.

Smack.

She jerked forward. Hudson caressed where he slapped.

"Don't make him ask you again," Hudson whispered as he cupped a breast from behind her. He stroked and pulled the nipple, offering it to Jagger. Jagger curled his finger toward her.

"I missed your body. I want to taste those beautiful, full breasts of yours, baby. Come to me."

As she moved, Hudson removed her panties. He shoved them down from her waist, and before she climbed up onto the bed and between Jagger's thighs, Hudson turned her face toward him and kissed her. He pressed his tongue in between her lips and ravaged her a moment before turning her back toward Jagger. Another hard smack to her ass, and she moaned as she climbed onto the bed.

Jagger immediately cupped her breasts as he widened his thighs. She was above him, and the feel of her body between his outstretched thighs, and their skin touching, brought on a surge of need and desire. It was so powerful, so instant, he needed everything he could get.

He stuck out his tongue and licked the tip. She watched him, with smoky eyes and parted wet lips.

"I told you what I wanted and where you belong back at the restaurant. Do you remember?" he asked.

She nodded her head. He thrust his hips upward. Hudson moved in behind her.

"Of course she remembers."

"Say it, Tia Rose. Where do you belong?"

Her cheeks turned a rosy shade of pink. He had to hide his smile. She was so sweet and shy. But she needed to know how badly they wanted her and how much she meant to them.

He gave her hips a squeeze.

"In between the both of you," she whispered.

He felt his desire surge. "And what? What completes the three of us?"

She hesitated.

"My exact words, baby," Jagger pushed.

"With you buried deep in my wet pussy and Hudson buried deep in my ass."

He smiled. "Good girl."

She moaned as Hudson pressed the lube to her anus and began to get her ass ready.

"Oh, God. Oh, my god, please."

"I know, baby. I know," Jagger whispered then pulled her down so he could kiss her.

She jerked a few times and even Jagger wondered what Hudson was doing to her. Jagger whispered into her ear.

"What is Hudson doing, baby? Tell me."

"He's pressing his fingers in and out of my ass. He's licking and biting my ass cheeks."

"Sounds fun. I'll have to try that later."

He stroked his finger against her pussy lips, but didn't press the digit up into her.

"Please, Jagger." She moaned as she began to thrust back against Hudson's fingers, while pushing harder against Jagger's fingers. But Jagger wouldn't finger fuck her yet.

"What is it, baby? What do you need?"

"Both of you."

"You have us," Hudson said from what sounded like clenched teeth.

"Inside me. Please, just get inside of me."

"With pleasure," Hudson whispered, then pulled his finger from her ass.

She gasped. "Here I come, baby," Hudson said and Tia Rose's eyes widened.

Jagger held her gaze. "Look at me. Don't turn away. Tell me what Hudson is doing."

"Oh, God. He's pushing into me."

"With what? His fingers, his cock?"

"Oh, God, Jagger, please. I can't take the dirty talk."

Smack.

"Oh!"

"You will take it. You love it, remember? You loved it in Paris and you'll love it here."

"Nice and easy, Tia Rose," Hudson said.

Jagger pressed a finger to her clit and Tia Rose moaned.

"Tell me what he's doing."

"Taking his sweet time sticking his cock into my ass," she stated firmly then pushed back. Hudson moaned as he gripped her around the waist.

"Fuck, baby. I could have hurt you." She was breathing heavy, as she leaned back against Hudson's chest.

Her breasts were in front of Jagger's face. Her pussy was sopping wet.

"You're a bad girl, Tia Rose. You're going to get a spanking for nearly hurting yourself," Jagger said as he plucked both nipples, making her squeal and move forward. Hudson thrust his cock into her ass, shoving her downward.

"Oh please. Please do something."

"I am," Hudson said through clenched teeth.

She reached down to press fingers to her own pussy. Jagger pulled them away.

"No. You can't get off by yourself. This pussy is mine right now and forever."

Tia Rose began to shake. "Oh, please, Jagger. Please touch me."

"Where? Where do you want him to touch you?" Hudson asked, getting into it, too.

"Down there. Please."

"Say it. Down where?"

"My pussy, damn it. I need you, Jagger. I need you inside me now. Fuck me already, will you?"

Her words aroused him immediately. He looked at Hudson, whose eyes were squinted and his desire apparent on his face.

"Oh, we're going to do more than that."

He adjusted his cock as Hudson held her upright. A nod of his head and Hudson lowered her body over Jagger's so that his cock pressed smoothly up into her slick cunt.

She took him in quickly and then began to move up and down.

"Oh!" She moaned and that was it. Something carnal and wild came over the three of them. It was instant, like some power surge of energy. Up and down, back and forth, they fucked in sync. Skin slapped against skin. The sound of Hudson's palm landing on her ass aroused Jagger to the point of no return. Hudson pinched her nipples as he pumped his hips up and down. Jagger thrust into her from behind and she moaned and then cried out their names.

Jagger followed and so did Hudson, growling as they exploded their essence into their woman.

The sound of their panting filled the bedroom, and Jagger's heart pounded inside of his chest.

He caressed her hair, as she laid her cheek against his chest.

"Ours. You're ours, Tia Rose, and you'll never disappear on us again."

* * * *

Tia Rose sat on the sofa in the living room, wearing the thick fluffy robe. It belonged to Jagger. She inhaled his cologne and the fresh smell of soap and men's shampoo that lingered on her hair. She looked out toward the city skyline, impressed beyond words about these two men and their penthouse.

They had made love several times to the wee hours of the morning. But now her lovers were answering some phone calls about closing a business deal, and making plans to take the next several days off. They wanted her to come to their vacation home in upstate New York. Situated on a lake, on a private twenty-acre lot of land. Hudson called it their relaxation retreat, where they would go out on their speedboat, go tubing, water skiing, and a whole bunch of other things. Things she knew nothing about. She couldn't help but wonder that they might find her too simple for their accustomed tastes. They were wealthy and she didn't know how wealthy. They said billionaires but really, she couldn't even imagine that amount of money. But it must be pretty damn much, because a penthouse this large, on Fifth Avenue in Manhattan went for millions.

She felt her belly quiver. They were Rolls-Royce and she was vintage. She came from Missouri, and from a broken family with so much screwed-up stuff, she was scarred for life. She couldn't even believe that she was here and had trusted them. Two men wanted her in their lives and in their beds. It wasn't even considered a normal relationship in the eyes of many people. What would her parents say?

Oh God, my father will destroy me with hurtful words and then demand more money. I hate them so much. They've done nothing but make me feel weak, and not good enough for anything or anyone.

The tears rolled down her cheeks.

"Tia Rose?"

She jerked around, and saw Jagger standing there, and looking concerned. Hudson was right behind him.

She quickly wiped the tears from her eyes as both men joined her on the couch. The cushion dipped down on either side of her and she held her hands on her lap. Her legs were tucked under her. She looked back out toward the scene before her. She always wondered what the city skyline might look like in an apartment this high and with such great views. Her apartment window looked at a brick wall and the garbage Dumpster down below.

"You're upset?" Jagger asked, and then placed a hand on her thighs.

Hudson moved his arm onto the back of the sofa and over her shoulders.

She eased back against both of them.

"This is such a beautiful view. You must love sitting here day or night. I've never seen such a view before."

Hudson gently glided his thumb up and down the base of her neck. Jagger moved his hand under her robe and against her skin.

His fingers caressed between her thighs, giving them a nudge, indicating for her to part them.

She turned to him as she slowly unfolded her legs as he wanted. She realized that she would do just about anything for them. Anything at all.

"This is the best view," he whispered as her robe parted by her thighs and her pussy came into view. She didn't have to look down to see, she felt the cool air against her heated mound.

"How often have you said that to a woman?" she asked before thinking. His fingers stopped their route and he moved them to her face.

"Baby, I've never said that to any woman. Don't you believe me, us, when we compliment you and tell you how good you make us feel?"

She swallowed the lump in her throat. She was such a scaredy-cat. She was so afraid of giving her all and to be burned, left behind, heartbroken, and used all over again. Not only had her parents done this to her but Salvador, her only lover, had as well.

She started to move, But Hudson's huge hand held her in place at her shoulder.

"Don't run away. Don't keep your fears inside. We want to know everything about you. We want to take care of you, Tia Rose. Please talk to us."

She turned toward Hudson. She could feel her eyes fill with tears but she would not cry. She was so scared, and yet so already in love with them that she couldn't let them know. They might think she was crazy or clingy or something. Maybe they thought she might want them for their money? Why did they want her when they could have any woman?

"I don't care about your money," she blurted out.

"What?" Jagger asked. She looked back and forth between them and leaned back as they both leaned forward.

"I don't care about how rich you are, about where you live, or what you even did to make all this money. I'm scared for a whole lot of reasons."

"Tell us some of those reasons," Hudson said.

"I have trust issues."

"Don't we all, baby." Jagger slowly began to undo the knot on her robe parting it the rest of the way.

"I've been hurt before and used. It was bad."

"Who was it? We'll kill him," Hudson said. She was naked in front of them. The fluffy robe fell to her sides. Tia Rose went to cross her legs but Jagger stopped her.

"Spread them for us. You're our woman now."

"That right there. Your words scare me."

"Scare you?"

"Entice me, get me all happy inside, but then there's this fear, and—"

Jagger placed his fingers against her swollen clit. She gasped and parted her lips. Hudson ran his thumb across her lower lip and then into her mouth. She sucked it, and then he lowered the wet thumb to her nipple and rubbed it back and forth. She felt her body tighten like a bow.

"Never be afraid of us, or the way we make you feel," Jagger told her as he maneuvered his fingers between her pussy lips. He thrust one finger up into her and she held his gaze until Hudson spoke.

"You don't think that we're scared?" Hudson asked.

"The two of you? No. Never." She shook her head.

Jagger added a second digit as Hudson pulled a little firmer on her nipple.

"Well, we do get scared. We've never felt this way about a woman. We've searched for you for so long, and then you showed up out of nowhere in Paris. It shocked us. You're perfect," Hudson said and then leaned down to kiss her lips.

When he released them, Jagger spoke. "We're glad that you don't care about our money, but because we're so well off, we can take care of you. We want you in our lives. Forever." Jagger began to increase his thrusts.

Hudson pulled off his robe and sat back down on the couch.

"You drive us wild. Forget about the past and the pain others have caused you, and focus on us. Just us," Hudson said.

She smiled at him and he smiled back.

"Get over here. I need you."

She looked at Jagger who pumped his fingers two more times and then pulled out of her. As she sat up and started to straddle Hudson's thighs, Jagger pulled her robe off.

She placed her hands on Hudson's shoulders and then felt Jagger move behind her. He was pulling off his robe as Hudson pulled her against him for a deep kiss.

The moment she pressed her ass back, she felt the tongue and teeth against her clit. She jerked but Hudson was there to hold her in position. A few strokes of his fingers and Jagger had both her pussy and her anus ready for cock. She couldn't wait. She wanted them inside her. That was where they both belonged.

"Take me inside of you, baby," Hudson said, and she reached under, gently stroked his cock, and then lifted up to align it with her pussy. Tia Rose eased her way down the thick, hard shaft. She held Hudson's gaze as Jagger played with her ass and got it ready for him.

The sight of Hudson's handsome face, crew-cut hair, and beautiful hazel eyes brought tears to her eyes.

"What's wrong?" he asked, giving her hips a squeeze. She felt Jagger's cock against her puckered hole.

"Nothing, Hudson. You're just so beautiful, and so is Jagger. I feel lucky."

"We're the lucky ones," Jagger said then kissed her shoulder as he wrapped an arm around her waist and slowly pushed through the tight rings. She lifted up with Hudson's help and then Jagger shoved in to the hilt.

She moaned and the lovemaking began. Not fast and wild, but slow and deep. It was torture of the best kind, and Tia Rose was nearly lost in the power of their connection.

"Ours, always. Right, Tia Rose?" Hudson asked as he cupped her breasts and pumped his hips upward. She tilted her head back as both men filled her.

"Yours, always," she said, and then they began to increase their speed. They pumped their hips and made love to her deeply, until all three of them were moaning and panting.

"Oh my God, this is incredible. Never like this, baby. Never." Jagger carried on and she knew exactly what he meant. This was amazing.

Hudson grabbed a hold of her shoulders and pressed them down as he pumped upward. She hugged his chest, wrapped her arms underneath him, tilting her ass back and upward, giving Jagger deeper penetration. In and out, up and down, they were wild, until they all moaned and exploded together as one.

Tia Rose held Hudson close. The three of them were locked together, trying to catch their breath and recover from their lovemaking.

"Nothing to worry about, baby. Nothing can come between us. This is destiny," Hudson said as he kissed her.

She smiled at the thought, even though deep in her gut she wasn't too sure. Something was bothering her. Perhaps it was that uneasy feeling after the break-in at her apartment? She wasn't sure. Or maybe the thought that someone was watching her? She willed the fears away. She wouldn't let ghosts ruin her time with Hudson and Jagger.

She would love them as long as they were together.

Chapter 10

Tia Rose listened carefully to the message on her cell phone. The voice was mumbled or disguised in some way, but the threat was clear. Someone wanted to hurt her. The voice said that they were coming for her, and very soon.

She swallowed hard, and felt her chest tighten with fear. Her first instinct was to call Hudson and Jagger. But one, they were upset with her for not going with them to their vacation home this morning, so she could give them ideas to decorate.

She had work and she also felt that it was important for them to know she enjoyed her job and needed to take things slow with them. Their talk of forever, and of course moving into their penthouse, kept her up most of last night. Secondly, she didn't want them involved with this situation. It could be her brother, Sean, trying to scare her before he showed up. There really wasn't anyone else who wanted to hurt her. Well, that she knew of.

"Hey, are you okay?" Alexa asked as she walked back to her desk. Tia Rose hadn't even heard her approach.

"Yes, I was daydreaming."

"Oh, who is he and does he have a brother?" Alexa asked and Tia Rose felt her cheeks go very hot. *Boy, did he have a brother, and he's mine, too.*

"That good, huh? I wish I could meet some handsome guy to whisk me away from this life. All I do is work," Alexa complained. The phone on her desk rang and she rolled her eyes and then answered it.

"It's for you. Line one."

"Oh, I'll take it inside my office."

Tia Rose walked to her desk and picked up the phone. That uncertain feeling was becoming worse.

"Hey, beautiful. Do you regret not taking a few days off and joining us?" Jagger asked. She smiled. His voice alone made everything instantly better.

"Not yet. Too much work to be done here."

"Well, you seriously have to start planning a vacation. We want to spend some quality time with you. What are you doing for lunch?"

"I have a meeting downtown, lunch included, and then I need to head back here to get some more designs done."

"Shit. Okay, well, how about we catch up tonight. We can meet you at your place?"

She really wanted them to. It would make her feel safer, especially after the phone call. Maybe she should tell Jagger about it? Maybe she should call the detectives?

"Tia? What's wrong?"

She took a deep breath, and then released it.

"Nothing. I guess stopping by would be great. I miss you both already."

"Ha! Told you that would happen. How is seven? Does that give you enough time?"

"Yes. That will be perfect. I'll call you later, or maybe text you during the meeting."

"Okay. Later, baby."

"Later, Jagger."

She hung up the phone, and smiled. Thoughts of seeing Jagger and Hudson tonight would be her sole focus. Not the threatening phone call.

* * * *

He waited outside the building. Lucky for him, it was getting dark and the cops wouldn't see him. That was if they were even around. Sean hadn't seen one yet. He knew his sister was in the office building. She took the bus and would be coming out soon. The moment he saw her, he was on the move. He figured it would be best if they walked and talked as opposed to taking the bus. He didn't want to be stuck like that in case he needed to bail.

Tia Rose walked along the sidewalk, and when he had the chance, he approached form behind.

"Hey, kid. We need to talk."

She swung around fast, and when he caught sight of her close up, he was stunned at how beautiful his sister was. She looked incredible.

"Sean? Holy shit. What are you doing here? I heard that the police are looking for you. What in the world?" He grabbed her and pulled her toward the side of the building and away from people.

"Hey, I need some help."

"No. I don't want to get involved. I haven't seen from you or heard from you in five years."

"I've been on my own for four of those five years."

"What? Dad and Mom said that you lived with them."

"They're fucking liars and thieves. I haven't lived with them in years. I needed to get out once you left. They went psycho." He looked away from her and hoped that she couldn't see the light scar by his eye. His father broke a vase and cut him while they fought the night Sean left.

"I couldn't handle the pain anymore, Tia."

"But you were with them. You sat there and let them treat me that way. I couldn't handle the pain either, or make up excuses anymore about my bruises and cuts. You didn't stand up for me. You were too busy shooting up or out drinking."

She tried to walk away but he stopped her by grabbing her arm.

"Tia, I fucked up. I was twenty years old and had nothing to my name. I left a year after you did. I got involved with some people who helped straighten me out."

"Really? Then how the hell did you wind up in an armed robbery in Missouri?"

He looked away and then back at her as he placed his hands in his jean pockets.

"I was there. Guilty by association. The crazy fuckers said they were going in for beer. Next thing I know, they're drawing guns, the storeowner is drawing his gun, and it's all a blaze of glory shit. I ducked and got the hell out of there."

"Then why did you run from the police? Why not turn yourself in and tell them your side of the story?"

"And they would believe some kid living on the streets."

She stared at him, and it made him feel lower than dirt.

"You're not a kid anymore, Sean. You're twenty-six years old. You need to start thinking about a future. Getting your ass straightened out."

"I fucked up, okay? I know I did. We didn't exactly come from a great home, Tia. How the fuck am I supposed to get anywhere if no one will hire me for a job?"

"I did. I went to school, I got my degree, and I worked three jobs. Two during the week, and one on the weekends. I got out and I survived."

"You think you're so much better? Then why the hell are you still sending them money? They talk about you like you were trash, and what about the fat jokes, the nastiness. If they were here right now, they'd hit you. Fuck, Dad would beat you until you were dead."

She stepped back, and he saw the tears in her eyes begin to fall down her cheeks.

He ran his hands through his hair.

"Fuck, Tia. I'm sorry. I'm desperate. Please. Just help me out. All I need is some money."

"You need to turn yourself in."

"And then what? Spend time in jail for a crime I didn't commit?"

"No, plead your case."

"With an appointed lawyer fresh out of law school? No, thank you. I like being free."

"I don't know what to tell you. Hey, did you call my cell phone and threaten me today?"

"What? No. What phone call? Someone threatened you?"

"Forget it. I need to go."

He grabbed her arm.

"Please, Tia. I need help."

She looked at him and he wished things had been different. He wished he could change the way their lives were, and how he hadn't stuck up for her when they were at home in Missouri.

She reached into her purse.

"Here's a hundred. It's all I have on me. I want you to think about turning yourself in. Hell, I'll go with you if you decide to do it."

He was shocked.

"What?"

"You heard me, Sean. I'll go with you to the police if you want to turn yourself in."

He lowered his eyes. He felt like such an asshole for getting into this situation, but he also felt relieved that his sister was willing to put the past aside and help him.

"Thanks, Tia. I'll think about it."

"I need to go."

"Okay." He watched her turn and leave. He couldn't believe it. She had been successful. She left the abuse and the bullshit behind her. Yet she still sent money to their parents, and he knew why. Tia was always sweet as could be. Even when she got hit for doing nothing wrong, she apologized and tried to not do anything to set her father off.

But it never worked. The man loved to hurt his children, and their mother was no different. A tear formed in his eye. Was it too late for him? Could he really turn himself in with Tia's help and start over? Maybe here with her?

He shook his head. He'd think about it. Maybe Tia Rose was right after all.

* * * *

Tia Rose got off the bus, and was running thirty minutes behind. Her encounter with her brother was weighing heavy on her heart. She just didn't know what to do about him. Should she have given him the hundred dollars? Should she have called the police or insisted that he go with her right then and there? She didn't know. What was done was done. But as she walked down the dark streets, three blocks from her home, that uneasy feeling hit her again. She felt as if someone were watching her. Sean said that he hadn't called her or threatened her over the phone. She believed him. She believed that he truly had changed somewhat.

He still needed to grow up and stop hanging around riffraff. She was shocked at the news that he left their parents home four years ago. She really needed to stop sending them money. The decision weighed heavy on her mind. Maybe if her brother turned himself in to the police and pleaded his case, she could give him some money, help him to find a job, and get on his feet. Their parents weren't there for him, just like they weren't for her.

She turned around quickly as she heard some noise coming from the alleyway she had just passed. Her nerves were getting the better of her. She was so damn shaky and skittish, that any noise was scaring her. She looked around frantically. The streets were quiet. There was someone walking in the opposite direction on the opposite side of the road. But she didn't feel safe. The reminder of the phone call, the feeling as if someone was watching her now, played her nerves like a violin. As she rounded the last corner, she heard something. She turned in a circle. No one was there. *Why am I freaking out? That call to me today was probably a wrong number. No one would attack me on my way home. This is a safe neighborhood.*

She looked ahead. One more block. She could see the entrance to her apartment. Was that Hudson and Jagger's car parked outside? She started to walk faster. Someone was definitely watching her.

She hurried and without thinking first, she stepped out into the roadway just as the light changed. A passing car honked loudly. She screamed and then covered her mouth. She looked around her as she stepped back, and waited for it to turn green. She looked behind her. No one was there. But she felt the hairs on the back of her neck rise. She was breathing heavily. Her heart felt as if it would jump from her chest and take off for safety without her body.

Turn green, turn green, turn green. Come on, Goddamn it!

The light changed and she practically ran down the block. Jagger and Hudson were there. The tears were streaming down her cheeks. She needed them. She needed the safety of their arms. She needed—

She threw herself into Hudson's embrace and he caught her. She didn't hear a word either one said. She felt them caressing her hair her back and asking what was wrong.

Oh, God, either I'm losing my mind, or someone really is trying to kill me.

* * * *

Hudson held Tia Rose tightly in his arms. He was concerned, to say the least, and one look at Jagger, who was scoping out the area, made him feel even more on edge. She was crying, and then as she settled down, wiped her tears from her eyes, she started laughing. It wasn't a normal type of laugh, but more of a nervous, scared reaction. She was trying to play off her fear now.

"Tia, what's wrong? Are you hurt?" Hudson asked. Jagger placed his hand on her shoulder from behind and she jumped. Then she shook her head.

"Oh, God, I swear I think I'm losing my mind." She tried to pull away. She reached into her purse. "I'm sorry I was late. God, I was walking along and I thought that someone was following me. I had this bad feeling and so I kept walking faster. I wasn't paying attention, I guess I scared myself stupid, and I nearly got hit by a car."

"What? Are you okay?" Hudson rubbed her arms, and stared down into her eyes. They were red and her chest was all blotchy. He could feel her shaking. She was definitely scared. She looked so petite right now, too, and that was when he noticed the sneakers.

She followed his line of sight.

"I always put on sneakers when I have to walk a lot of blocks. Most New Yorkers do that."

"I know, baby. You just look so petite."

She smiled, and then she hugged him. Jagger moved closer, and pushed the hair from her face.

"You're shaking," Jagger said.

She turned to him and pulled back from Hudson.

She looked around them. She still seemed upset.

"Let's go inside. Please." She grabbed Hudson's hand and pulled him with her. Her grip was firm and he looked at Jagger. Jagger shrugged his shoulders.

As soon as they made it to the top floor of her apartment, Jagger stopped them.

"Wait. What is that?" he asked, moving in front of Tia and Hudson. Hudson pulled Tia back.

"What's wrong?" she asked.

Jagger reached for the doorknob. The lock was broken.

"Shit, someone broke in again."

"What?" She tried to push forward but Hudson held her firmly.

Jagger pushed the door open, and the moment he did, Hudson wished Tia hadn't been right there to see. The place was destroyed.

The words "die bitch," "whore," and other obscene words were spray-painted on the walls. Antique furniture was destroyed, all her clothing scattered, including lingerie.

"Oh, God. Someone is trying to kill me."

"What?" Hudson asked.

Jagger grabbed her arm and turned her toward him.

"Has someone been threatening you?"

She was quiet, the tears rolled down her cheeks.

She nodded her head.

"Goddamn it." Jagger raised his voice.

Hudson was immediately angry with Tia. How come she hadn't told them? Why didn't she trust them? Someone could have really been following her home right now. They could have hurt her.

"Oh, God. I can't believe this. Who would want to kill me?"

Hudson pulled her against his chest, Jagger locked gazes with his brother.

"Call Jett and Flynn. Have them call Cash and Zane."

"Call who? No, call the police," she stated.

"We're taking care of you. You're coming home with us, and we're going to get to the bottom of this. So no more keeping things to yourself. No more handling things on your own. You got it?" Hudson asked her. And he knew he raised his voice. He knew he was getting through to her, as her eyes widened like saucers and she nodded her head.

Jagger was talking quickly on the cell phone, and then he called the police, as well as well as Leo Deluca, Toni's cousin who was a detective. They were going to need their friends help on this. No one was going to hurt their woman.

Chapter 11

Tia Rose was in the back room at The Phantom nightclub, a place owned by good friends of Hudson and Jagger. She felt so sick to her stomach, and especially the fact that the police and detectives thought her brother Sean might be a suspect. She hadn't told them that she saw him tonight. She truly didn't believe that he was responsible. But then, after they left her apartment building, she felt guilty for not telling Hudson and Jagger the truth. Their friends were helping, but she felt so vulnerable. She trusted Hudson and Jagger. But these friends of theirs were very wealthy, too, and she wasn't sure about them.

"Hey, I brought you this. I figured you might need one." Jett and Flynn's manager, Adelina, approached with two snifters of brandy. Tia smiled and nodded a thank-you.

Adelina seemed nice. She was drop-dead gorgeous, too, and both Jett and Flynn always seemed to be looking for her presence. She wondered if they were an item. But then they didn't touch her or caress her skin, or show any sign of romantic involvement. Something told Tia they liked her, and Adelina liked them. It was just an assumption, but there was definitely something going on.

"I know you're probably pretty scared right now. But you have the best guys on your side."

"I don't know any of you. I don't know who would want to hurt me either. I feel bad, getting everyone involved in my problems."

Adelina smiled.

"Hey, these guys are all like brothers. They stick together, and it will always be like that."

"They've all been friends for that long?"

"Since elementary school. You see Nash and Riker were Federal agents. They got out and were involved in numerous investment opportunities that made them rich. They own Hidden Treasures. Ever been there?"

"No. I don't really like to go out to clubs. Honestly, I'm always working."

"Yeah, tell me about it. Sometimes I feel like I live here."

"Anyway, Emerson and Stone, the two over there wearing the blue and black T-shirts, are crazy wild. Or at least they were until they met their woman, Toni. She owns Bliss, in SoHo."

"Oh God, that place is so well known. I didn't know a woman owned the place."

"Yeah. Toni is really nice, too. You met Cash and Zane. They were the ones along with Flynn and Jett that helped to locate you."

Tia swallowed hard.

"I was shocked when Hudson and Jagger found me. I thought I would never see them again."

Adelina smiled and then leaned closer.

"Honey, those two talked about you for weeks. They all meet here Wednesday or Thursday nights for poker. It's a tradition."

"That's very nice to have such close friends. What do you think they're talking about now?"

Adelina looked toward them.

"They're probably figuring out a way to protect you, and get you to Hudson and Jagger's penthouse without you being followed. That should be simple enough. I'm sure Cash and Zane will find out soon who's following you and threatening you. They're really good at that and own a security firm. Their girlfriend, Chiara, owns Costiano's."

"Wow. Their friends landed them some very professional and independent women." She knew she sounded defeated, and maybe even jealous. What was she? A designer in a company where she didn't come close to making six figures. Bethany had been making six figures.

"Hey, I hear you're a great designer—"

Tia Rose stood up. "I'm so sorry. I just thought of something. I need to text someone."

"Oh, okay. I'll leave you alone. I'll go see if the guys need anything."

"Thank you for the brandy," Tia Rose said to Adelina. She smiled and then headed out of the room.

Tia pulled out her cell phone. And when she did, she saw the text message.

Salvador? What the hell do you want?

She didn't read it. She just texted Alexa. Alexa was always on Facebook, and she also assisted Bethany in setting up her Facebook page. Maybe they could see where Bethany was and when her latest posts were.

She texted quickly, then went back to her main page on her cell to read the text from Salvador.

Hey, sweet buns. I was thinking about you. I miss you and was hoping to see you tonight. I stopped by, and there was some security tape on your door. One of the neighbors said you were robbed. Call me if you need a place to stay. I'd love you in my bed. It's always open.

"Who are you texting?"

Tia jumped as Jagger approached her from behind.

"Oh, no one. Just answering some messages. Nothing." She repeated as she placed the phone behind her and swallowed hard. Why she felt guilty for the text from Salvador, she didn't know. But she didn't want Jagger to see it. He and Hudson could take the message the wrong way.

He eyed her suspiciously.

"Are you sure that you told us and the police about everyone you thought could want to hurt you?"

He asked her and she thought about Salvador. He didn't want to kill her. He had already broken her heart, and now Leza probably dumped him, and he was in need of a booty call.

She nodded her head.

Then her phone buzzed, indicating that another text came in.

She didn't move.

"Aren't you going to answer that?"

"I can later."

"Answer it now. I'll wait," he said.

Jagger had such a way about him. He was demanding, bossy, and so downright confident and powerful when he spoke, she automatically wanted to do as he said. Which definitely made her body react too. *Spread your thighs. Show me your wet, pretty, little pussy.* His words in the bedroom came crashing back to mind.

She gulped and her phone buzzed again.

Now his expression grew firmer. "Answer it."

She didn't want to argue. She looked down at her cell phone and was relieved that it was Alexa. She opened it up. "It's Alexa. From work."

He didn't say a word. She read the text. It said that Bethany's Facebook page had a post from two hours ago. She was in Brazil on a beach, and she wasn't alone.

Tia sighed in relief. Okay. So Bethany was not after her.

She looked at Jagger as her phone buzzed again.

"Where are you, sweet buns? I know that you don't have anyone. You're alone, with no family or friends in New York. I'm waiting in bed for you. Hurry."

"Asshole," she said under her breath.

"What?"

"Oh, did I say that out loud? Forget it. It's nothing."

"Hey, we're ready to go. Just a few more questions for Tia Rose," Hudson said.

"Sure," Tia replied and began to walk toward Hudson and the guys. Jagger grabbed her wrist and the phone.

She looked up toward him. He appeared angry and she could see that small vein by his eye, pulsate.

"No secrets. We're here for you. Who texted you?"

She couldn't lie to him. And as Hudson approached and looked upset, she told them.

"So you thought that this Bethany could be the one threatening you?" Hudson asked.

"I checked with Alexa. Bethany is in Brazil."

"Well, that's easy enough to confirm. We'll take care of that," Cash stated.

"Any other texts?" Jagger pushed.

"Not any that I would like to discuss right now," she whispered.

"Why not?"

"They're personal, and not important." He held her gaze and she hoped that he would drop it for now. When they were alone, she would tell him and Hudson all about Salvador.

"Okay. We're ready then," Hudson said and she waited while they planned her departure from the club, through the back exit door.

* * * *

Cash and Zane drove a black SUV with tinted windows. Tia was in the back seat between him and Hudson. Jagger wanted to know who texted her, but she held the cell phone tight as it went off again.

Nash and Riker followed in another car behind them. They would go in the underground garage at the penthouse, and get into a private, delivery elevator by Jameson. Hudson already spoke to him.

She fidgeted with the phone and when it went off again, she placed it under her arms to try and hide the buzzing.

"Okay. Who the fuck is texting you? And I don't want any lies or bullshit." Jagger raised his voice and Tia Rose jumped.

She must have seen his dark expression even though the light in the SUV was dim. Up front Cash and Zane remained looking forward.

"It's no one of importance, Jagger."

"Well, they keep texting you, so who is it?" Hudson asked.

She took a deep breath and released a sigh.

"Salvador."

"Who the fuck is Salvador?" Jagger asked.

She was silent a moment. "No one of importance."

"Then why does he keep texting you?"

"He's my ex-boyfriend, Jagger, okay. He found out about the break-in and he texted me."

"What's his last name?" Zane asked from the front seat.

"Why?" she asked.

"Answer him, and then we'll deal with the texts when we get home," Jagger replied.

"He has nothing to do with this," she added.

"How do you know? All bases have to be covered. How many times do you read shit in the paper about ex-boyfriends stalking their ex-girlfriends and then trying to kill them?" Zane stated from the front seat.

"What's the fucker's name, Tia Rose?" Jagger asked again.

"You're not helping, Zane," Tia stated firmly, and then she told them his last name.

"Send it to Jett and Flynn, as well as Riker and Nash," Hudson added.

Tia Rose leaned back in the seat and crossed her arms in front of her chest.

"Watch that attitude. It will cost you later," Jagger warned her and she shot him a look.

He held his expression and could see that she knew he was getting angry. Why didn't she realize that they were both concerned for her? What was she not telling them? Could she possibly have an idea who wanted to hurt her, yet she was holding back telling them? What about this Salvador asshole? How long were they involved? Was it serious? Did he hurt her? Could he want her back? Was she thinking it over?

Jagger ran his hands through his hair. He released an annoyed sigh and then looked at Tia Rose again. He was jealous and fearful and totally on edge.

"Salvador is a jackass. He means nothing. If you want to know the truth, he dumped me. He cheated on me and hooked up with some bimbo model. I was never good enough for him, and he always put me down, just like my parents had. His texts mean nothing. He's looking for a damn booty call," she blurted out.

"What? That fucker texted you for sex tonight?" Jagger raised his voice.

"We're here. And before this gets a bit uncomfortable, may I suggest taking care of this upstairs when the three of you are alone," Cash said as he pulled into the underground garage.

Zane turned in his seat and looked toward them. An obvious smirk on his face.

"And where you can punish her privately," Zane stated.

Hudson and Jagger both sat forward and locked gazes. Tia Rose was in for it the moment they got her upstairs.

* * * *

Tia Rose took off her shoes and sat down on the couch as she waited for Cash, Zane, Riker, and Nash to discuss the next steps for Hudson and Jagger to take. They felt pretty confident with the security in the building, and the fact that the only way upstairs to their penthouse was by private elevator, and Jameson was working tonight. He wouldn't let anyone through without Jagger and Hudson's approval.

As the men said good-bye and told her to listen to her men, she let out an uneasy sigh. Leaning her head back, she closed her eyes and so many thoughts flooded her brain.

Someone wanted her dead. Her brother wanted her help, and he was considered a suspect. She should really tell Hudson and Jagger about seeing him tonight. But what would they say about giving him money? She nibbled her bottom lip.

She really believed that her brother was telling her the truth. Every bit of her gut instincts kicked in and she thought he was being sincere. She hoped that he turned himself in. If he did, and he came to her for help again, then she would do it.

She trusted her gut. Especially tonight when she heard noises and felt the goose bumps along her neck and hairline. She knew she was being watched and followed. Then to come home to her trashed apartment was crazy. She was so grateful that Hudson and Jagger were there, waiting for her, and that they helped handle the situation.

I don't have any clothes, no laptop to work from. I need to call work and speak with the Sinclairs. What am I going to do?

She covered her face with her hands.

"Tia, we need to talk," Hudson stated, and his voice had her sitting up to face him. Jagger leaned against the post in the living room a few feet away. It was like he was keeping his distance. Maybe he didn't trust her? Could she blame him? She hadn't been completely honest with him. She needed to come clean.

"Yes, we do," she replied.

"First of all, tell us about Salvador. Is he a threat to what we have between the three of us?"

She immediately shook her head.

"Tell the truth. Do you still love him? You still want him?" Jagger asked from afar.

She stared at Jagger.

"No. I never loved him. I cared for him, but he used me, and dumped me for someone beautiful and thin. I met him when I was naïve and stupid, and felt that he was perfect, which made me feel real."

"When did you meet him, and why was he perfect?" Hudson asked, approaching the couch and sitting down beside her.

She took a deep breath and held his gaze. Hudson and his beautiful hazel eyes watched her with intensity. It made every part of her body come alive. She loved him, and she loved Jagger.

She leaned back and released a long sigh.

She couldn't look at them as she spoke. She feared seeing their displeasure, or perhaps their true feelings toward her. Even now, after making love, and sharing so much of herself with them, she feared being abandoned.

"You should know that before I left for Paris, my life was terrible. I lived with an understanding and acceptance that I was invisible."

"Invisible?" Hudson asked softly.

She looked at him, but only a moment. It was one thing to admit to defeat, to hating whom she was to herself, and another to say it aloud and admit such deep feelings of negativity.

"Invisible, fat, unattractive. Unworthy of being noticed, cared for, or even thought of. I was a nobody, who allowed people to walk all over me, and put me down. I had no spine, no fight in me to defend myself or to feel anything but disgust for who I was."

"Jesus, Tia Rose. Why did you feel that way? You're so beautiful. How could no one notice you?" Hudson asked, as he laid his hand over hers.

She pulled it away and looked away from him.

"You don't understand. I was all alone. Even when I was surrounded by coworkers and other people, I was alone. I couldn't stand up for myself. I know a lot of it has to do with the abuse I sustained as a child, but still, I left. I made the decision to take off and live."

"Abuse? Who abused you?" Jagger asked, walking closer.

She lowered her eyes, clasped her hands on her lap and rung her fingers together. "My parents were abusive. They still are." She chuckled.

"They're the ones you've been sending money to each month?" Jagger asked.

She looked up at him, shocked that he knew about that. "How did you—"

"You dropped a piece of paper from the money transfer in the hotel room in Paris. That's how we were able to locate you," he told her.

She didn't have the strength to be angry. What did it matter?

"Why do you keep sending them money if they treated you so badly?"

She felt the tear roll down her cheek. "I guess I hoped one day, that they would love me."

"Oh God. They don't deserve your love, your attention, and especially your hard-earned money," Jagger told her.

"You don't know my dad, Jagger. His words hurt worse than his fists."

"Fuck. He'll never lay a hand on you again. You're through sending money to them, you hear me?" Hudson raised his voice.

"It's not that easy, Hudson," she replied.

"It is that easy. They're cut off. You don't need them," Jagger added.

"I do need them. I don't have anyone in this world. I can't stand being alone anymore. I can't take it. Even if they are abusive, and mean, and hate me, they're there. They call to confirm the money transfer. They call," she said as her voice cracked.

Hudson took her hand into his own. Jagger knelt down on the rug in front of her and placed his hand on her knee. "You're not alone anymore. You have us."

"We'll take care of you." Hudson added.

She shook her head and stood up. She stepped away from them.

"No. I can't believe you. I can't trust anyone. People lie and they use you. Salvador did. He told me that I was perfect, and then wanted to change me. You'll do the same."

Jagger pulled her into his arms. "No, we won't, because you are perfect. You're all woman, and you're our woman. I don't want skin and bones and a supermodel with no brains. I want tits and ass, and attitude. I want a woman who knows what she wants and asks for it. You're strong, you're gorgeous, and you're ours." He hugged her to him.

She cried as his words sunk in and Hudson joined them. He hugged her from behind and caressed her back.

"That asshole Salvador never cared. We do," Hudson said, as he turned her toward him. They stood in front of her, so strong, and handsome. Her two lovers. The two men who owned her heart and soul.

"He doesn't matter to me. He's history."

"If he calls you again, I'm going to hunt him down and kick his ass. Do you understand me?" Jagger stated.

She felt her belly quiver at his declaration. He placed his hand against her cheek.

"Tell us what changed before Paris," Hudson said.

She took an unsteady breath and released it.

"I was tired of being walked all over. Salvador dumped me that morning after standing me up the night before. He told me that he had sex with Leza, a model, and that I was the coldest fuck he ever had."

"Dick wad," Jagger whispered, and she chuckled.

"I told him that I wasn't cold, and that it was him and his little penis."

Hudson chuckled and so did Jagger.

"Then on my way to work, in my not so happy mood, I got something brown on my skirt."

They walked her over toward the couch again to sit down, and she explained everything that happened that day. They listened attentively, and they smiled at her show of independence and making a stand.

"Are you certain that this woman, Bethany, couldn't be after you?" Hudson asked. "I mean you embarrassed her, got her fired, and probably ruined her reputation."

"I thought about it. But Alexa, she's the other person who texted me at The Phantom, said that Bethany's Facebook page showed her in Brazil."

"That doesn't mean anything. People can fake that stuff."

"And what about your brother, Sean? Could he be trying to scare you enough to maybe show up and pretend to want to help you?" Hudson asked.

She lowered her eyes and stared at her hands. She needed to tell them the truth.

"Tia Rose?" Jagger said her name.

"Um, I kind of saw him already."

"What? Where and when?" Jagger asked.

"Before I headed home from the business meeting at the restaurant. He was waiting by the building for me."

"Did he try to hurt you or threaten you?" Jagger asked. She shook her head.

"No, Jagger, he actually needed help. He said that he was set up, and that he needed money."

"You talked to him?" Jagger asked.

"You gave him money, Tia?" Hudson asked.

"I believe what he said. He was in the wrong place at the wrong time. He left my parents place a year after I did because he couldn't take the abuse. He said that he was at the place that was robbed, but he wasn't involved."

"Then why didn't he turn himself in?" Jagger asked.

"I asked him to do that. To turn himself in. I gave him a hundred dollars, and told him that I would help him if he went to the police."

"Why? Why would you do that after all the abuse and what occurred in your house back in Missouri?" Jagger asked.

"Because he's my brother, and if we don't have each other, then it's over. The family, the bloodline and ties, end there. I had to give it a shot. I believe him. I think he's telling the truth."

"And if he isn't? If he lied to your face to gain your trust and then rob you, hurt you, and leave you for dead, then what?" Jagger asked her.

She waited a moment, and thought about his words.

"Then I died trying to keep the last bit of hope for a family alive."

Both men released annoyed sighs and stared at her. She couldn't look at them.

"Do you believe that we care about you?" Jagger asked, and then stood up.

She looked up, her head reaching her shoulders, as she took in the sight of his huge presence. She still couldn't get over how big they both were. It appealed to her in so many ways.

"Answer him," Hudson stated, making her look back toward him. She couldn't describe the love, the desire to please them that was running through her system.

The sight of their muscles, their chiseled faces, carved from stone like Greek gods, had every part of her body quivering for their touch and attention.

She licked her lips. She had to take this chance. She had to be honest. She had to give them everything one last time in her life, and if they failed her, if they left her, then life was over. This was it.

She clasped Hudson's hand, and then reached for Jagger's and took his.

She stood up and so did Hudson.

Looking up at both men, her heart racing, her legs about to give out from shaking with fear of what they might say to her admittance, but she said it anyway.

"I…I love you both."

She gulped the lump of emotion in her throat, felt her nose clog up and a cry about to escape her throat as she waited for their response.

Hudson wrapped an arm around her waist. Jagger cupped her cheek in his palm. She gasped, as she look up at them.

"I love you, too," Jagger whispered.

"I loved you the moment I laid eyes on you in Paris. A goddess from the Renaissance right before my eyes. I knew that you would be mine," Hudson told her.

She smiled as she sniffled. "Please don't abandon me. Please don't lie to me and tell me I'm beautiful, and that you love my body, when you don't. Please don't break my heart. I would die if you—"

Jagger placed his fingers over her lips.

"You are beautiful. Your eyes are the most gorgeous shade of green I have ever seen."

"Your body is perfect. We're big men, Tia Rose, and we want to feel our woman in our arms, against our skin, and know that as we make love deeply and with all our heart, that you can handle it," Hudson added.

"I need you both. Right now."

"And we need you," Jagger said. He took her hand, Hudson kept his hand on her shoulder, and they walked out of the living room and toward the bedroom.

Tia Rose felt such a weight lift off of her shoulders. To know that they loved her, too, made her accept their control, their power, and their desire to keep her safe. No one ever loved her before, and now she had two men to love her and keep her safe.

* * * *

Jagger turned her around to face the bed, as Hudson got undressed first.

He unzipped her dress and slowly pushed the material down her body. He let his hands linger on her shoulder, as he leaned down to kiss her skin.

"Hudson and I had a rough start in life. We understand about abuse and neglect. Our mother had to work multiple jobs to take care of twin babies when our father left her. He had been abusive, too. We lived in poverty for quite some time," Jagger whispered, and then kissed her skin again. He undid her bra, and she let her arms hang so that the material fell right off of her.

He continued to massage her shoulders, then her back and her ass, pushing her panties off of her body, as Hudson walked in front of her.

Hudson cupped her breasts and leaned forward to take a taste of her nipple. Jagger began to remove his clothing.

"Our mom worked hard to keep food on the table, and steer us clear of gangs and drugs. We worked our way through high school and college and started out working in small firms around the city," Hudson said, his warm breath colliding against her sensitive nipple. She felt the tiny bud harden as she closed her eyes, and tried to have a verbal conversation.

"Your mom must have been so proud of you. Is she still alive?" She tilted her head back and moaned, as Hudson sucked her nipple and part of her breast into his mouth.

"Yes, and happily involved in a ménage relationship, too."

She jerked up and looked at Hudson.

"Really?"

The strong, thick arm came around her midsection and Jagger hugged her from behind.

"Yes, really. Mom, Richie, and Daniel are perfect together. You'll meet them when they return from vacationing. Mom's going to adore you," Jagger told her as he kissed along her ear, then pulled the lobe between his teeth and tugged.

"Spread your thighs, baby. I want to see what's mine," Hudson said, and she slowly spread her feet. As Hudson lifted one of her feet and placed it on the bed behind him. Jagger held her snugly, so she could lean back against him and not fall.

The moment Hudson's fingers began to play with her pussy lips, she felt her pussy cream, and a small eruption overcome her.

"You're so responsive to our touch. I love it, baby, and I love you," Hudson said, and then leaned forward and kissed her softly on the lips.

Jagger simultaneously thrust his thick, hard cock against the crack of her ass.

Hudson pulled back, and stood up. He slowly stepped back, and lay on the bed with his legs hanging off the side.

"Come on up here and ride me, baby. I need you now." His arms were wide open as Jagger released his hold, and she moved on top of Hudson. Her heart soared in adoration, and then she felt Jagger's hands caress her cheeks. He was spreading them, and squeezing them and she felt his large, solid thighs tap against her backside.

"You know that we have to punish you for your behavior earlier, right?" Jagger asked.

She swung her head to the right to look at him as Hudson aligned his cock with her cunt and pushed upward.

She gasped.

Hudson grabbed a handful of her hair and held her tight. It was such a dominant move, and it turned her on way more than she should have been turned on. Her pussy pulsated, and Hudson thrust upward.

"Oh," she moaned.

Jagger continued to massage and squeeze her ass cheeks.

"You never hold back with us. Never lie to us or try to take care of things yourself. That's what we're here for. We're going to take care of you and love you. The sooner you get that and accept it, the better our lives will be. And if that fucking ex-boyfriend calls or texts you again, you'd better tell one of us. Do you understand?"

Hudson thrust upward, as he held her hair in his hand.

"Yes. Oh, God, yes, Jagger, I promise."

Jagger reached down and caressed her cheek. He ran his finger along her jaw and then between her parted lips.

"Good girl. Now, brace yourself, baby. First I'm going to spank this ass, and then I'm going to fuck it."

"Oh yes, Jagger, please. I want you to. I promise to never lie and always be yours. Please," she begged, feeling the tears burn behind her eyes.

Smack.

Smack.

Hudson released her hair and pulled her down to his chest. As he spread his thighs, her ass stuck out further, and her thighs widened.

She felt Jagger press a finger to her very wet cunt, and then continue to spank her.

Smack. Three. Smack. Four.

"Oh!" She moaned as he pressed two digits up into her pussy, and began a fast pumping motion. She felt her entire body tighten, and then he moved his fingers from her cunt to her ass. He pressed through the tight rings, making her grip onto Hudson and moan against his shoulder.

Smack, smack, smack, smack.

She couldn't take it as she wiggled and then absorbed the scent of Hudson's cologne. The feel of Jagger's extra large, wide palm colliding against her skin sent waves of pleasure through her body. She sucked on Hudson's skin and he thrust upward as the hand came down hard on her ass one, two, three times in a row.

"Fuck, she's sucking my neck. Oh, God, it feels so fucking good. I'm going to come." Hudson grunted.

Large hands gripped her hips and then she felt the fingers leave her ass, giving her a moment reprieve from the electrifying sensations.

"Oh, God!" she yelled as her pussy clenched and released more cream. She gasped when the mushroom top penetrated her well-lubricated ass and filled her up. She bit into Hudson's neck, making him grunt and then grab onto her and thrust upward.

Up and down, in and out, the two men filled her with cock.

Smack.

Smack.

She began to shake and shiver.

"Fuck, yeah. Oh, sweet mother, I'm coming." Hudson grunted against her as he held her tightly in his arms. He thrust upward, and she felt his cock hit her womb, while Jagger continued to thrust into her ass. She wanted to scream it felt so incredible and wild, but she couldn't. She wanted more. She wanted more.

"I'm there, baby, come with me," Jagger said, as Hudson released her and she sat up and shoved back against Jagger.

"Holy fuck, Tia. What are you doing?" he stated and then grabbed onto her shoulders and she pumped her hips and ass backward against Jagger's cock. His hands practically covered her shoulders and his fingertips reached the top of her breasts.

"Oh, God, oh, my God." She shook and exploded on top of Hudson.

Jagger grabbed her hair, held her in place, and pumped his hips three more times until he found his release.

"Mine. Holy God, you're mine, Tia Rose, and I fucking love you." He panted for air, and she slowly lowered to Hudson's embrace. She caught sight of Hudson's hazel eyes, and the most beautiful sight. His smile. She prayed that they would never leave her. She wanted to feel this way forever, and hoped that nothing and no one would ever come between them, not even the person set out to kill her.

Chapter 12

It had been three days since the break-in at her apartment. Tia Rose wanted to return to work, but Hudson and Jagger didn't see how they could ensure her safety. At least if they knew who was after her, they could maybe find them first. The detectives thought that Sean had something to do with it. Tia Rose insisted that he didn't.

Hudson was on the phone with Adelina. She had called with the idea of helping Tia Rose shop for new clothes since her things were destroyed in her apartment. As much as he and Hudson loved keeping their woman naked, she couldn't exactly go out wearing one of their robes. They were huge on her anyway.

Jagger could hear what sounded like Tia raising her voice. He walked toward the bedroom, but not before he locked gazes with Hudson who must have heard her raised voice as well.

"Adelina, this sounds perfect. We'll meet you there in an hour. Thank you," Hudson said and then hung up the phone and followed Jagger to the bedroom door.

"I don't really care that you think I'm fat, ugly and wish I was never born. In fact, why don't we pretend that I don't exist, and you can stop calling me? I'm dead to you, and have been for quite some time," Tia Rose said into her cell phone as she typed away on the computer.

"I know there's no money in the account. I closed it out. I'm done with you. If you ever call me again or harass me in any way, I'll call the police, and I'll tell them about your little secret operation in the fields. Moonshine is still illegal, and especially when selling it to minors. Yeah, I'll do it, and I'll also charge you with assault, abuse, and neglect. The statute of limitations is not quite up.

"I've already been to hell. That was my life having you both as parents, and the abuse I took over all those years. I'm done now. Good-bye forever." She hit the end call button, tossed the phone onto the bed, and growled with her teeth clenched.

Jagger felt proud of her. She had finally told her parents to leave her alone.

"That's my girl," Hudson said. She swung around, her beautiful green eyes as big as saucers.

"I didn't know you were listening."

"It was hard not to," Jagger teased as he approached and pulled her into his arms. She grabbed onto his forearms and hugged him.

"I'm sorry that you both had to hear that. I can't believe he's been calling me continuously for the past twenty-four hours."

"What? And you didn't tell us?" Hudson asked, with his eyebrows furrowed.

"I needed to do this on my own, Hudson. I knew you would want to help, but it was me who needed to tell them off and cut the ties. I can't believe I just did that."

"How does it feel?" Jagger asked her.

"Amazing. I feel like a weight has been lifted off my shoulders. Yet I kind of feel bad."

"What? Are you crazy?" Jagger asked her.

Hudson stepped closer and placed his hand against her cheek.

"Not crazy, just as sweet as can be. Our woman has a forgiving and kind soul."

"Our woman better stay close by our sides, or she might wind up in trouble."

Tia Rose chuckled. "On another note. I really do need to get back to work. Has Cash or Zane come up with anything yet?"

"No. But we are working on a plan for you to go back. Adelina called, and she wants to go shopping with you. She suggested it, since you don't have any clothing," Hudson told her.

She stepped back from Jagger's arms and placed her hands on her hips. She looked so damn sexy in his robe. And even sexier naked.

"And how did you respond to her idea?" she asked.

Jagger reached for the belt on the robe and tugged it, making it come undone. Tia Rose hadn't even removed her hands from her hips. She knew Jagger's moves by now as she smiled up at him.

"I didn't give my answer. I prefer you like this." He cupped her breast, causing the nipples to push forward over the space between his thumb and pointer. He used his thumb to cress the tips as he held her gaze.

"I need clothes, Jagger."

He leaned down and licked one tip and then the other.

"I need you. All the time." He blew warm breath over each tip.

"Jagger, please," she begged of him. He looked at Hudson, who raised his eyebrows. "She does need clothes."

"Okay, but not a lot, and no panties. I'll just rip them anyway," He teased her and then raised his eyebrows up and down. She chuckled and smiled before he pulled her against him and kissed her.

* * * *

It was getting late when Adelina and Tia Rose had finally finished shopping. They decided to head to The Phantom for some drinks and food. As they arrived, the men spoke with their friends, and Adelina and Tia walked to the ladies' room.

"Thank you so much for going shopping with me. I couldn't believe that you convinced Hudson and Jagger to let me go."

"Are you kidding me? I know how important your job is to you. I also love to shop and you needed a new wardrobe."

"Yeah, I can't believe that Hudson and Jagger paid for everything. I can't seem to get used to the fact that they're so wealthy. I like having my own money, and buying things myself."

They continued to talk while they took care of their business in the ladies' room, and then Tia emerged, and began to wash her hands.

"You should let them take care of you, but also remain independent to an extent. If they're anything like their friends, they'll accept that you want to continue to work and have your career. After all, they had to work very hard for their money," Adelina said as she began washing her hands.

"What about Jett and Flynn? Would they allow their woman to have a career?" she asked. Adelina shot her head up to look at Tia Rose, and Tia smiled.

"I don't think so. They don't do commitments and serious relationships. They like no-strings-attached women."

"How does that sit with you, being their club manager and all?" Tia Rose asked, and Adelina placed her hands on her hips and gave Tia a sideways expression.

"What are you thinking?"

"That you like them and they like you."

"No. They don't have any feelings like that for me."

"And how do you feel about them?"

She shrugged her shoulders.

"I've been here for three years. If something was going to happen, it would have by now. Let's head back."

"Okay. I didn't mean to pry. I could just tell that they like you, Adelina. They watch you when you're not looking," she told her.

Adelina smiled. "Thanks, Tia."

They headed back out to the club and through the very crowded dance floor.

Tia felt a hand grip hers and start pulling her in the opposite direction.

"Hey!" she exclaimed, until she realized that it was Sean.

She saw Adelina still making her way through the crowd, and with the lights flashing and the music blaring, she knew that she wouldn't hear her.

Her brother glanced back at her. "I need to talk to you."

She allowed him to bring her back toward the direction they came from.

"Sean, what's going on? We should stay here so that my—"

"Boyfriends? Don't worry. I know. I saw them with you. It's creepy."

"It's not creepy. I love them and they love me."

"Please, just step outside with me. I've been waiting to talk to you. Someone has been following you. I saw the police at your apartment. Did someone break in?" he asked, as they exited the back door.

They were standing outside when she stopped him from bringing her further away from the door. She was scared. She had become so reliant on Hudson and Jagger to make her feel safe, and even now, with them just inside, she was scared.

"Sean, who did you see?"

"I don't know who the person is. But I saw them again tonight. They were watching Hudson and Jagger while they were talking at the bar."

Her brother was rambling. He seemed genuinely upset.

She reached for his hand.

"Come back inside with me. Hudson and Jagger can help you."

He pulled back. "They won't be able to keep me out of jail. The detectives will bust me for that armed robbery."

"But you said you didn't do anything. You didn't have the weapon and you didn't steal, correct?" She stepped down further from the back door.

Her brother was pacing. "I don't have any money for an attorney. They'll hang me."

"I told you that I would help you." She reached out her hand. "Trust me and I'll help you, Sean. I promise. Just take my hand."

The back door to the club swung open. Hudson, Jagger, Jett, Flynn, and some other guys came barreling through.

"Tia Rose, what the hell is going on? We were worried."

Sean took a few steps back, but Tia grabbed his sleeve. She looked at Hudson as he and Jagger took position beside her.

"This is my brother Sean. Sean, meet Hudson and Jagger Ross, and Jett ad Flynn Greyson."

"Tia, please. I don't think they can help me."

"Tell us what's going on. If you're Tia's brother and you need help, we're here for you," Hudson said, as he took a step toward Sean.

"You can trust them, Sean. I sure do," she replied.

Tia began to explain about her brother's problem, and the fact that the police thought he was involved. Sean told them all about what happened that night, and then Jett and Flynn said they could probably help.

"Let's head inside and talk. It's pretty dark out here," Jett suggested.

"Yeah, and someone has been following Tia Rose. I saw them," Sean told them.

"What? Who did you see? Did you get a good look, a description?" Jagger asked.

Tia Rose felt the pain the moment she heard the shot. She fell forward against Hudson, who caught her. Everyone ducked, but Flynn and Jett, as well as the other two men behind them. They drew their weapons as Tia placed her hand over her shoulder and chest. The pain radiated from her back to her front. She lifted her hand in what felt like slow motion, and when she looked down it was covered in blood.

"Oh, God, she's hit. Someone shot her," Hudson stated, as Jagger shoved open the back door and Hudson carried her inside. They laid her down on the floor as Jagger pulled out his phone. She could hear them yelling. They were calling for an ambulance.

I've been shot. Oh, God, it hurts.

She began to panic and tried to move, escape from more gunshots, but Hudson held her against him. She looked at him. The fear in his eyes, the anger instantly told her that this was real, and she was hurt badly.

Hudson placed his hand over the wound.

"Ow!" The pain struck her hard.

"There's so much blood," Hudson whispered and pressed something harder against the spot the pain radiated from.

"Oh, God. They shot me. Who was it? I'm scared, Hudson. I'm scared." She felt the panicked feeling worsen, but as she went to move, her body wouldn't allow it. She felt cold and unbalanced.

"Shh, baby, it's okay. You're safe in here. Help is on the way."

"They'll get away. They'll come after you and Jagger."

"Shh, baby, please, let us handle this. Just lie still," Hudson said and then looked up at Jagger.

She saw their faces, their eyes, and the concern.

"It hurts," she whispered, closing her eyes as she tried to drown out the pain and the fear she had. There was so much going on around her. It felt like they were mumbling. And then she started shaking.

"Here, cover her with this, apply pressure to that wound," Adelina stated.

Hudson placed something else over the wound. She felt the pain get worse and now she was shaking. Her teeth were clattering.

"She's going into shock. Where's that fucking ambulance?" Jagger yelled.

"Hold on, Tia Rose. Please, baby, hold on."

* * * *

Tia Rose blinked her eyes open. Flashes of strangers smiling down at her, talking to her, trying to ease her mind as they moved her around. She complained that it hurt to move, but they did it anyway. Hudson's and Jagger's voices echoed around the strange voices.

There were lights and loud music, bumps as they moved her, and then she closed her eyes, trying to get through the pain.

She saw black and heard nothing until she felt her body bump onto something. She tried blinking her eyes to see clearer, but she couldn't. There were bits and pieces of things, as she would lose focus and then see again.

The light was so bright. There were all these sounds and people were talking. She saw blue and white coats and then a bright light. The small flashlight illuminated her eyes.

"Tia Rose, can you hear me? I'm Dr. Lang." She blinked harder, but her lids felt so heavy.

"I shot." She said the words but it sounded so strange. Was she speaking?

"We gave you something to help with the pain. You're going into surgery, Tia. The bullet is lodged under your chest bone."

"Hudson, Jagger, Sean."

* * * *

"This is insane. You're telling us that the crazy bitch from work, Bethany, shot Tia Rose? She's the one who destroyed her apartment and has been stalking her?" Jagger asked Flynn and the detectives.

"Yes. She's mentally unstable. Had been under a physician's care for years," Flynn told Hudson and Jagger. All their friends were there, waiting to hear about Tia Rose.

"We caught her down the block. She was raging about killing Tia and seeking her revenge. When the other detectives got to her apartment, the place was filled with pictures of Tia Rose. It appeared as if Bethany had become obsessed with her," Detective Leo DeLuca, Toni's cousin, informed them.

"We thought she was out of the country. Tia mentioned a picture on Facebook," Hudson added.

"A fake. Bethany was good at conniving people. She had her therapist fooled, and her family." Leo explained more about what was found in Bethany's apartment, including a list of other people at Malone's she planned on killing, including Dante Perrone.

"Holy shit." Jagger ran his hands through his crew-cut hair and stared toward the doorway where the doctor would hopefully, soon, emerge.

"Tia Rose has to pull through this. She's fought for so much," he added.

Hudson placed his hand on his brother's shoulder. "She will and then we'll take care of her. No one will ever hurt her again."

"Jett, did you find out about Tia's brother? Is the situation fixable?" Hudson asked him. Jagger still wasn't sure how he felt about Tia's brother. Could the man be trusted? Did he really want to get help and straighten his ass out? Was he involved with the armed robbery and did he lie to Tia? Jett, Flynn, Cash, and Zane were doing their best to find out. Jagger felt so compelled to protect her, and especially now, after being shot.

"The detectives are examining the video surveillance tapes from the robbery. We'll know more soon, but for right now, Sean is being held until the investigation is complete. He was so worried about his sister. He's totally cooperating, so that's a good thing," Leo told them.

"We appreciate your help with this."

Jett gave Hudson a tap to his shoulder and nodded toward the doorway. A grim-looking doctor, who appeared exhausted, stood there.

"Is the family of Tia Rose present?" he asked.

"We're it. We're her family," Hudson stated.

"And where are Hudson, Jagger, and Sean?" he asked.

"I'm Jagger, and this is my brother, Hudson. Sean isn't here yet," Jagger stated, not wanting to go into great detail about the current situation.

"Okay, Tia Rose is in recovery now. She's a very strong young woman. The bullet lodged in her chest bone. It appears that she was shot from behind, the bullet penetrated through to the front of her body where the chest and shoulder bone meet. Lucky for her, it was in a good position for me to remove it without causing further damage. X-rays show no splintering of the surrounding bone, but there was severe tissue, and cartilage damage. I did my best to clean that up, repair what I could, and quickly seal the wound. She currently has a breathing tube inserted to assist her in breathing normally. I hope to remove this sooner than later, but she was very panicked and I don't want to take the chance of her injuring herself further. Right now, she is sedated, and the best thing for her to do is rest. It was quite the severe injury, and she's lucky to be alive."

"Will she recover completely?" Hudson asked.

"She's a strong woman. As long as she rests and takes her time healing, she should be fine. She has a lot of resting to do. I don't expect her to leave here too quickly."

"Can we see her?" Jagger asked.

"I will have the nurse come for you to visit Tia Rose when she's settled in ICU."

"Thank you, Doctor. Thank you very much for everything," Hudson said and shook his hand. Jagger then did the same thing. The doctor turned around and left the waiting room. It seemed like a sigh of relief swept through the room. One glance, and Jagger saw all their friends. All concerned, and all right there being supportive and caring for them, like a family truly was.

Jagger looked at Hudson.

"She's going to make it, Hudson. Our woman is strong."

Hudson smiled. "Thank God, because right now, I feel like I'm going to pass out." Hudson fell down into the seat and covered his face with his hands. Jagger placed his hand on his shoulder and squeezed it.

"We'll get through this, and before you know it, Tia Rose will be home with us, and our new life will begin together."

Chapter 13

"Jagger, why are you carrying me?" Tia Rose asked, as she reached under her thighs to make sure that her dress was in place and nothing was showing underneath.

"Because we've been carrying you around for the last three months, and we like it," Hudson said as he caressed her hair, while she laid her head on Jagger's shoulder.

"But we have a house full of guests arriving and there's so much to be done."

"Our friends know that we love you and adore you. Besides, they would carry their women around, too, if she needed pampering."

She was going to argue, but truth be told, she loved them carrying her around as if she were light as a feather. Their big strong muscles had held her close and kept her safe since returning home to their penthouse after the hospital. Now, they were all celebrating with their friends at a weekend-long barbeque at Hudson and Jagger's vacation home in the Adirondacks.

The house was spectacular, and it sat on a private lake with a beautiful beach they would enjoy all weekend long.

"There they are. What took you three so long?" Jett asked as he popped a cherry tomato into his mouth and smiled.

"They were insisting on carrying me still."

"Get used to it, princess. You feel best in my arms and not at a distance," Jagger told her, as he gently set her feet down onto the floor and then kissed her softly.

She shook her head, but felt her cheeks warm from his public show of affection.

"Well, I don't blame them at all. If you were my woman, I would be carrying you everywhere as well, and keeping you as close as possible," Flynn stated. She smiled, and then looked at Adelina.

Adelina was placing the steaks onto a large platter to be cooked. They locked gazes and Tia Rose winked at her. She hoped that Jett and Flynn made a move sooner than later. Those two had to be the most stubborn men around. Over the last few months, Adelina and Tia had become good friends, as well as Toni, Chiara, and Chastity. They had formed a bond between the five of them, and Tia Rose felt so lucky. She never had any good friends, just like she never had any family. As they made their way outside, she spotted Sean, standing by the grill cooking up some fresh clams. He had a huge smile on his face as he spoke with Nash and Riker, while Emerson and Stone held Toni between them as they joked around about something.

Sean had come so far and with the help of all their new friends, the charges were dropped against Sean. Chiara got Sean a job in her company. He was working from the bottom up, and currently worked in the factory where they brought in the fresh fish to then create all the packaged items her company was known for. He loved it, and she was so very proud of him.

Hudson approached and placed his hands on her shoulders. She leaned back against him as they joined the conversation. Jagger smiled at her, and then ran his knuckles gently against her cheek. She smiled softly, thinking about what her two men told her, the day she awoke in the hospital. She would never forget it, and she knew that she would love them forever.

"You're our everything, Tia Rose. Before we met you, we thought that achieving money and power made us everything," Hudson told her.

"We worked so hard to make our money and to never feel the struggles of not knowing where the next meal was again, or not being able to afford a pair of shoes, or a blanket to keep warm," Jagger added.

"We wanted so much and focused so much on our journey to getting rich and never being poor, yet ultimately we were still empty, in here." Hudson pointed to his heart.

"Meeting you changed everything for us. You're more important than money, than power, or anything materialistic we could ever buy or want." Jagger held her gaze with his gorgeous hazel eyes.

"Our journey to fortune wasn't the billions we made and continue to make. Our fortune is you, Tia Rose. We love you," Hudson said.

"We love you more than anything. Stay with us forever. Be our woman, our treasure, our everything?" Jagger asked

"And we promise to give you the world," Hudson added.

"I love you both so much. I thought I would never be loved or cared for by anyone, but the two of you opened up my world and gave me a new perspective on life. I want to be your woman. But I'm the fortunate one. I have two perfect men who love me and the family I always wanted."

Tia smiled at the memory, and absorbed the laughter around them, and the simple normalcy of having a family and enjoying their company. Life couldn't get any better than this. She felt complete for the first time in her life. There were no more negative thoughts. No more fears of not being good enough. Just lots and lots of happiness and love, and she owed it to her two sexy billionaire boyfriends, whom she would love for the rest of her life and with all her heart.

THE END

WWW.DIXIELYNNDWYER.COM

ABOUT THE AUTHOR

People seem to be more interested in my name than where I get my ideas for my stories from. So I might as well share the story behind my name with all my readers.

My momma was born and raised in New Orleans. At the age of twenty, she met and fell in love with an Irishman named Patrick Riley Dwyer. Needless to say, the family was a bit taken aback by this as they hoped she would marry a family friend. It was a modern day arranged marriage kind of thing and my momma downright refused.

Being that my momma's families were descendents of the original English speaking Southerners, they wanted the family blood line to stay pure. They were wealthy and my father's family was poor.

Despite attempts by my grandpapa to make Patrick leave and destroy the love between them, my parents married. They recently celebrated their sixtieth wedding anniversary.

I am one of six children born to Patrick and Lynn Dwyer. I am a combination of both Irish and a true Southern belle. With a name like Dixie Lynn Dwyer it's no wonder why people are curious about my name.

Just as my parents had a love story of their own, I grew up intrigued by the lifestyles of others. My imagination as well as my need to stray from the straight and narrow made me into the woman I am today.

For all titles by Dixie Lynn Dwyer, please visit
www.bookstrand.com/dixie-lynn-dwyer

Siren Publishing, Inc.
www.SirenPublishing.com

Lightning Source UK Ltd.
Milton Keynes UK
UKOW06f1630070316

269743UK00001B/332/P